DR. QUINN
Medicine Woman

QUEEN OF THE MAY

Don't miss the previous book in this series
by Colleen O'Shaughnessy McKenna:

Dr. Quinn, Medicine Woman: New Friends

DR. QUINN
Medicine Woman

QUEEN OF THE MAY

An original novel by Colleen O'Shaughnessy McKenna
Based on characters from *Dr. Quinn, Medicine Woman*

SCHOLASTIC INC.
New York Toronto London Auckland Sydney

Photo credits: Cover, Peter Kredenser. Insert, page 1 (top): Charles Bush, (bottom): Peter Kredenser; page 2 (top and bottom): Peter Kredenser; page 3 (top): Peter Kredenser, (bottom): Michael Yarish; page 4 (top and bottom): Cliff Lipson; page 5 (top): Charles Bush, (bottom): Peter Kredenser; page 6 (top): Peter Kredenser, (bottom): Cliff Lipson; page 7 (top): Charles Bush, (bottom): Cliff Lipson; page 8 (top): Cliff Lipson, (bottom): Charles Bush.

ISBN 0-590-60373-6

12 11 10 9 8 7 6 5 4 3 2 1   6 7 8 9/9 0 1/0

Printed in the U.S.A.   40

First Scholastic printing, March 1996

This book is dedicated to all of the wonderful doctors in Pittsburgh, Pennsylvania.

—C.O.M.

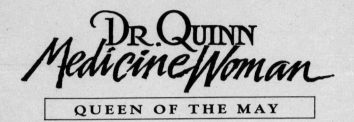

QUEEN OF THE MAY

1

The late April sun beat down, flashing diamonds in the water as the wind swept across the blue stream. Colleen closed her eyes and smiled. It was hard to imagine that heaven could be any more pleasant than this.

"I'm so glad you brought us here today, Dr. Mike," Colleen said. She opened her eyes and reached across the quilt to squeeze Michaela Quinn's hand. "I've missed you!"

Dr. Mike patted Colleen's hand. "Oh, I've missed you, too, Colleen. It's been weeks since we've been on the front porch, just catching up. I had no idea a mild case of the grippe could have such an impact. I've treated more than thirty people since it hit Colorado Springs."

Colleen shook back her hair. "Well, the worst is over. I'm glad you were able to leave Miss Dorothy in charge of the clinic for a few hours. This is the longest we've been together in weeks."

Dr. Mike glanced at the buggy. "Those toma-

1

toes won't wait. You and Becky were a big help to me today at the reservation. They sure appreciated the plants we delivered." Dr. Mike lifted her face up to the sun. "I haven't been outside like this in such a long time. The sun feels wonderful."

"You've been working *twelve hours* a day at the clinic for the past week, Dr. Mike," Colleen pointed out. "If you don't let others help out for a few hours, you'll come down with the grippe yourself!"

"Sounds like good medical advice to me, Colleen." Dr. Mike laughed. "But we should be heading back soon. Do you want another sandwich?"

"No thanks. Becky?"

"No thanks," mumbled Becky from beneath her arm. She was lying facedown on the soft, worn quilt. "But I do want to stay here by the stream forever."

"If only we could." Dr. Mike pointed toward a large blue spruce. "Look at the wingspan of that hawk."

"Spring is my favorite season," Colleen decided. She bent down, unfastened her shoes, tugged off her stockings, and dipped both feet into the cool stream.

"Colleen, we have to leave in five minutes, okay?" Dr. Mike drew her knees up to her chest, breathing in the fresh air. "I can hardly wait to start the garden. Sully promised me fresh flowers in every room all through the summer."

"I'll help plant," offered Colleen. "Unless Sully wants to do this all by himself." Colleen was so happy that Dr. Mike and Sully were finally married, but sometimes she wondered how crowded it must feel to have three children underfoot during the honeymoon year. Colleen smiled. Her older brother, Matthew, lived in the old homestead, so lately he came for supper only a few nights a week. But Colleen and Brian were always there. Oh well, thought Colleen, so far Dr. Mike and Sully seemed as happy as could be.

Colleen dipped her fingers into the water and sprinkled it across the back of Becky's neck. "Hey, sleepyhead, Becky! Wake up! You're missing the most perfect day!"

Becky stood up and stretched. "This has been great, Dr. Mike. Hey, Colleen, what do you think the rest of the class is doing right now? Probably arithmetic!"

Colleen laughed. "I prefer counting the birds, then subtracting the butterflies. Who needs to be indoors on a day like this? Thanks for letting us play hooky today, Dr. Mike."

"Hooky?" cried Dr. Mike. "We were doing a good deed for the Cheyenne! I had no idea my mother would ship me so many tomato plants from Boston."

"I wish we could visit the Cheyenne every day," said Becky.

3

"Reverend Johnson might not agree." Dr. Mike laughed. She stood up and brushed off her long skirt. "Girls, let's pack up. Miss Dorothy has her hands full at the clinic. Mr. Bray was brought in last night, full of complaints."

"Mr. Bray is so crabby," said Becky. "And his daughter Abigail was the sweetest person on earth. Why, she . . ."

Becky's head jerked up. She slapped her hand over her mouth as her cheeks reddened. "Oh, excuse me, Dr. Mike."

Colleen noticed the pink that flooded Dr. Mike's cheeks as well as Becky's. Abigail Bray had been Sully's first wife. She had died, along with their infant son, during childbirth.

"Don't apologize, Becky," Dr. Mike said easily. "Abigail must have been a beautiful person, inside and out."

"Like you, Dr. Mike," Colleen said quickly.

Dr. Mike smiled as she gathered up the picnic basket. "Time to get back."

Colleen grabbed Dr. Mike's hand. "Five more minutes, please?"

"I have to get back to the clinic, Colleen."

Colleen dried off her feet and slipped them back into her stockings and shoes. Was Dr. Mike really worried about the patients, or upset at the mention of Abigail?

Becky tugged on the end of the quilt. "Hurry

up, Colleen. Dr. Mike doesn't have any extra minutes anymore. Not only is she a married lady, but she has a clinic full up with the grippe."

Colleen sighed. Becky was joking, but she was telling the truth as well. Dr. Mike was so busy lately. Almost too busy. Spring would be a great season to catch up with each other.

"The Cheyenne sure were grateful for the tomato plants," Colleen said. She wanted the afternoon to end on a cheerful note. "Cloud Dancing's wife gave me two skinned rabbits. I'll make a stew for supper tonight."

Dr. Mike flashed Colleen an appreciative smile. "You are such a big help, Colleen. I don't know what I'd do without you."

"I love helping out." Colleen meant it, too. Years before, when her real mother was alive, Colleen had helped run the boardinghouse. It seemed only natural now to help Dr. Mike with the cooking and at the clinic. And now that Sully and Dr. Mike were married, there was even more to do.

Colleen and Becky folded the quilt and followed Dr. Mike to the buggy, which stood in the shade of a fir tree.

"We'll have to write Grandmother Quinn to tell her how grateful the reservation was for the tomato plants," said Colleen. "She'll be pleased."

Dr. Mike laughed, then shook her head. "My

mother is not *easily* pleased. Now, if I decided to pack all of you up and head back east, she would be *thrilled*."

"Maybe stories about the Cheyenne scare her," offered Colleen. "Boston is so far from Colorado Springs."

Becky nudged Colleen. "The Cheyenne scare a lot of people. Richard told me that if the Cheyenne tried to kidnap me, he'd organize a search party."

Colleen glanced up at Dr. Mike, then frowned at Becky. "Richard doesn't know what he's talking about, Becky."

"The Cheyenne are not our enemies, Becky," explained Dr. Mike.

"They're our friends," insisted Colleen. "When we gave them the tomato plants, they gave us some coneflower seedlings."

Becky nodded. "I like sunflowers."

Colleen put the quilt in the back of the buggy. "The coneflower is special. Dr. Mike, isn't that the flower Cloud Dancing used in the tea he gave you when you were so sick?"

Dr. Mike nodded. "Yes. The purple coneflower. Acts like quinine. A flower both pretty and practical."

"Just like you, Dr. Mike." Becky giggled.

"All aboard, girls," Dr. Mike called out.

"I wish we could come back here tomorrow," Colleen said as she climbed up beside Dr. Mike.

"You'll be back at school tomorrow, girls."

6

Colleen rolled her eyes at Becky. "Tomorrow will be a *long* day."

"Oh?" said Dr. Mike. "Big test tomorrow?"

Colleen shook her head. "Big *con-test* tomorrow."

Dr. Mike looked interested. "Spelling bee?"

"I wish," Becky said. "At least you can study for those. Tomorrow we're having nominations for May queen. Of course, Miss Alice O'Connor, the belle of our school, is already planning her campaign to win. A little boy told me yesterday that Alice promised him a bag of candy if he voted for her."

"Is that allowed?" Dr. Mike asked.

"No!" stated Becky. "Some people get locked up for bribery."

Dr. Mike picked up the reins. "Alice must really want to win."

Colleen smiled at Dr. Mike. Some ladies in town would have spent the next ten minutes ripping Alice to shreds. Not Dr. Mike.

"Now, when is May Day being celebrated? Friday?"

"*Saturday*, Dr. Mike." Colleen had told Dr. Mike about the festival a dozen times, but there had always been interruptions. Colleen sighed. Sully, Matthew, Brian, patients . . . everyone needed Dr. Mike. Since Colleen was the oldest child at home, she was the one who ended up waiting.

Becky grinned over at Dr. Mike. "We've been studying all about England, so Reverend Johnson thought it would be interesting to have the real festival, complete with a Maypole, dancers with ribbon streamers, food tables . . ."

"Morris dancers," added Colleen. "I think there will be about six of them. One will be dressed as Robin Hood, another as Friar Tuck, another as Maid Marian. Of course, Richard should dance the part of the Fool. A perfect match."

"Richard wouldn't have to *pretend* very hard, would he?" Becky remarked. "He is so funny sometimes. We also have to elect a May queen and king. Blake Russell will be elected king." Becky paused, putting her hand over her heart. "Blake Russell *is* a king."

"Becky!" Colleen gently elbowed her friend. "I don't believe you said that! Wasn't it just yesterday that you swore you didn't have a crush on him?"

"Must have been somebody who just *looked* like me," insisted Becky. "Besides, Blake is so nice to everyone, he should be king."

"Is he new in town?" asked Dr. Quinn.

"Blake's dad works for the stage line," Becky reported. "They moved here from Denver, and before that, Philadelphia. Blake's very nice to little kids, he can do a backwards flip, and he's allergic to strawberries." Becky paused. "He's very good in history, helps his dad shoe the horses, and

. . . maybe that's all I've found out about him."

"He sounds very nice," commented Dr. Mike. "Is he the boy Brian has been talking about so much lately?"

Colleen nodded. "Blake walks home with us a lot. Brian loves to hear stories about the stage line." Colleen loved to hear the stories herself. Or maybe it was just listening to the way Blake told them. He had a hundred voices inside of him.

"Well, when this grippe leaves town, we'll have to invite his family over for supper," said Dr. Mike, as she turned down a rutted dirt lane.

"Invite me, too." Becky laughed.

Colleen smiled, not a bit surprised. The fact was, ever since Blake moved to town three months ago, every girl over the age of ten had had a crush on him. Not only was he nice, but his eyes were a blue so clear and bright you thought you were looking into a piece of perfect sky every time you saw them.

"King Blake." Becky gave a deep sigh, still gazing out into space. Colleen and Dr. Mike smiled at each other.

"Surely other boys are going to be nominated," said Dr. Mike.

Becky nodded. "Of course. Richard nominates himself for everything. And Lindsay will nominate her big brother, Paul. But trust me, Dr. Mike, Blake will win by a landslide."

"I'm looking forward to the festival," said Dr.

9

Mike. "Colleen, we'll have to make sure you have a dress."

"My mother has almost finished making mine. Hey, did I mention Blake has a dimple, Dr. Mike?" asked Becky. "Just one. God probably realized *two* dimples would result in too much perfection on one human face."

Dr. Mike raised an eyebrow. "This Blake is quite a catch."

Colleen nodded. "Nobody's caught him yet."

"Maybe by May Day." Becky laughed.

Dr. Mike slowed the horses and leaned over, studying each girl. "Oh, no. Just as I suspected."

Colleen's hand flew to her face. "What?"

Becky leaned closer. "What's wrong?"

Dr. Mike sighed. "I was afraid this might happen. You both have a terrible case of it!"

Becky looked worried. "The grippe?"

"Worse!"

"What?" both girls cried at once.

"Spring fever!"

2

Colleen and Becky were thrilled to be diagnosed with a case of spring fever. For the rest of the buggy ride home, they told Dr. Mike everything they knew about May Day.

"We'll be voting for the king and queen tomorrow," said Becky, "but they won't be announced until Saturday. Reverend wants to keep us in suspense. But right after the king and queen get crowned, the Maypole dancers start dancing around."

"We need ten or twelve girls for the Maypole dancers, a couple more to act out a skit for the Morris dancers, and, of course, the queen." Becky sighed. "One queen. Too bad Blake couldn't be like King Henry the Eighth and have *lots* of queens."

Dr. Mike laughed. "King Henry usually killed his queen to make way for the new one, Becky."

Becky sighed again. "Blake wouldn't. He'd let us all live in separate towers."

"You've been in the sun too long, Becky." Colleen ran her fingers across the top of her skirt. "Reverend asked the older boys to build a Maypole for the dancers to circle around. He said they could carve a fancy ball for the top, and we could use it every year. The Maypole dancers each hold a long ribbon streamer and they dance around the Maypole."

"I remember. The dance is in honor of Flora, the goddess of spring," said Dr. Mike.

"And all the dancers get to wear flower crowns in their hair," explained Becky. "Plus, we give a basket of flowers to someone we love the most." Becky raised her eyebrows. "I hope Blake has a big, big house to hold all the baskets he'll get."

Colleen was about to mention that Blake had a small house, but she didn't want to have to explain how she knew that. Dr. Mike might not understand if Colleen told her she had stopped by Blake's house for a lemonade the other day. Blake had insisted they stop when Colleen complained about feeling dizzy. When Mrs. Russell was told, she insisted Colleen sit on the porch swing for five minutes and sip something cool before heading home. Mrs. Russell was very nice. She called Colleen Beth at least four times. For some reason, this had upset Blake. Maybe Beth had been Blake's old girlfriend when they lived in Denver.

I should have asked him about that, thought Colleen. That afternoon, Blake had carried her books all the way to her fence, in case her dizziness returned.

"Reverend wants us to make paper baskets, just like they did in England years ago," continued Becky.

Colleen studied Dr. Mike's profile. She was so pretty, even covered with buggy dust and weary from lack of sleep. "Dr. Mike, did you ever dance around a Maypole?"

"No, but my four older sisters did. One year my oldest sister, Rebecca, was May queen, and ten years later my sister Marjorie was crowned." Dr. Mike's smile shrank. "Marjorie told me I should volunteer as the May*pole* since I was so thin that year."

"So, when *were* you May queen?" asked Becky.

"I wasn't."

"You're kidding," sputtered Becky. "You're so pretty!"

Dr. Mike smiled. "Thank you."

"You would have been the most beautiful May queen of all!" Colleen announced proudly.

"Thanks, Colleen. I'm afraid my head was always too far into a book to even think about such things. As the youngest of five daughters, I'm sure my father was relieved when I *didn't* show any interest in being queen of the May."

"Well, Miss Alice O'Connor sure has an interest," declared Becky. "She hasn't stopped talking about it all week."

"May Day sounds like fun," said Dr. Mike. "I think you should both run for queen. You're both so nice to everyone."

"It's not that simple, Dr. Mike," explained Becky. "Alice and her ladies-in-waiting don't want any competition. I think it's safer if Colleen and I refuse to run for May queen. We can be Maypole dancers instead."

"Girls, don't refuse to run."

"But Dr. Mike, we don't *want* to be queen — right, Colleen?"

"Alice is bound to win, Dr. Mike," agreed Colleen.

"Sometimes you have to take a chance on things," Dr. Mike said softly. She turned down the lane to Becky's farm. "You'll never have a second chance to be thirteen years old."

Becky grunted. "Thank goodness!"

Colleen held onto the back of the seat as they bumped down the lane. She could feel Dr. Mike's eyes on her. Being a Maypole dancer with Becky would be fun. Besides, Alice was busy telling everyone who stopped to listen that she just *had* to be queen. Alice O'Connor usually got what she wanted. She would be pretty sore if another girl wore the rose crown.

"Hey, Colleen, wake up!" Becky shook Colleen's shoulder. "I was saying that as soon as we get to school tomorrow, we'll tell Reverend that we *def-*

14

initely want to be Maypole dancers. Let the other girls fight over being queen."

Colleen wasn't sure if she should agree or not. Part of her wanted to do whatever Becky wanted. Having a best friend took a certain amount of compromise. But Colleen could feel Dr. Mike's eyes on her. Did Dr. Mike want Colleen to take a chance on being queen? Was it because Dr. Mike never had the chance, or because Dr. Mike wanted Colleen to have a taste of everything?

"Right, Colleen?" Becky had hopped from the buggy and was waiting for an answer. "We'll tell Reverend right away."

"All right," Colleen said slowly.

"See you tomorrow!" called Becky as she raced across the grass.

Dr. Mike turned the buggy around and headed for home. "So, it's settled then."

"Yes," said Colleen. "Worrying about May queen is a waste of time, Ma. Besides, Alice will win. Becky really wants us to be Maypole dancers together."

Dr. Mike nodded. "Alice wants the crown, Becky wants to be a dancer. I was just wondering what you wanted, Colleen."

Colleen shrugged, then smiled. "I'm so happy right now, I don't want a thing."

Dr. Mike's laughter rose above the clomping of

the horses. "It wouldn't be spring if you didn't have at least one wish, Colleen."

"Maybe I'll think of one later," said Colleen. "When my spring fever gets even worse."

"You're a funny one," said Dr. Mike softly.

For the rest of the buggy ride home, the two of them held onto their smiles.

3

A light rain was falling Wednesday morning, so Dr. Mike offered to take Brian and Colleen to school in the buggy. Colleen was excited. She never minded getting a little wet, but she loved the idea of talking to Dr. Mike all the way to school. After supper last night, Sully told Colleen that he thought she should run for May queen if someone nominated her. "Nobody loves springtime more than you and Michaela," he said. "Don't turn your back on an adventure."

The buggy ride to school would give Colleen a chance to talk to Dr. Mike and find out what she *really* thought about Colleen's plan to refuse to run for May queen.

"It's getting late. Let's get going," Dr. Mike called out from the front yard. "Brian, don't forget your lunch."

"Coming!" Brian shot out the front door and raced to the barn.

"Colleen, I don't know if I'll be late for supper,"

said Dr. Mike. "I'll have to see how last night went."

"Okay. Dr. Mike, do you think I should run for May queen if I get nominated?" Colleen hiked up her skirt and put one leg in the buggy. "Just for the adventure of it all?"

"Sure. You have such a nice group of friends at the school," said Dr. Mike. "And being queen is only for a day. It's not as if the queen had to give royal balls and collect taxes!"

Colleen laughed. "Or marry the king."

Before Colleen could get her other leg into the buggy, Horace Bing came riding up to the door of the barn. "Thank goodness you're here. Miss Dorothy said you were coming in late. Something's wrong with the baby."

Dr. Mike hurried out of the barn. "Oh, Horace, not the grippe . . ."

"No, no, thank goodness," Horace said quickly. "But something distressing, just the same. Myra and I tried everything to make her stop hiccuping, but nothing's working."

"Hiccuping?" whispered Colleen. She stepped out of the buggy. Mr. Bing had come to interrupt Dr. Mike for a case of the hiccups? Didn't people realize Dr. Mike needed to rest and take care of her *own* family?

"Tell me about her symptoms, Horace," Dr. Mike said calmly.

Colleen groaned and leaned against the buggy.

18

Mr. Bing ran a whole telegraph office by himself. Couldn't he handle this situation by himself, too? How hard could a hiccuping baby be?

"Mr. Bing, did you try putting a bag over her head?" asked Brian. "Or plug her nose? Stand her on her head!"

Horace looked horrified. "Glory, no, Brian! She's a baby! They're very breakable. Myra and I walked her around and around the table all night long, but nothing worked. Any second now, she's gonna hiccup her heart right up out of her throat!"

"I'm sure she'll be fine," Colleen said, stepping closer to stand beside Dr. Mike. The morning drizzle was settling on everyone's hair and coats. If they stood there much longer, they'd all be down with the grippe. Colleen slid her hand into Dr. Mike's and gave it a squeeze. *Hurry up and tell him to go home*, Colleen's squeeze said. *I have to talk to you, Dr. Mike.*

"She's in no danger, Horace," Dr. Mike assured him. "A baby still needs to get used to her parts."

"What if one of her parts is busted?" asked Horace. "Oh, I know it's asking a lot of you, Dr. Mike. I've seen how full up the clinic is, but Myra is scared stiff."

"I'm sure it's not serious, Horace," explained Dr. Mike. She gave a small smile down at Colleen and Brian. "I promised to drive the children to school, and . . ."

Horace's face washed grayer than the settling

19

fog. "Oh, sure. I'll . . . I'll . . ." He swallowed. "We'll be okay."

Colleen took her hand away and sighed. Mr. Bing wasn't trying to steal minutes away. It wasn't his fault so much was going on right now. "It's okay. Go with Mr. Bing, Ma."

By the way Mr. Bing was clenching the reins, Colleen knew he wasn't going to rest till Dr. Mike drove into town and checked his baby.

"Come on, Brian. Let's walk," suggested Colleen. "We won't melt."

"Children, make sure you dry off in front of the stove once you get there," called Dr. Mike.

"Bye, Ma!" Brian zoomed past Colleen. "Rain can't catch me."

Colleen waved and headed down the road. She could hear Mr. Bing talking from his horse as he followed Dr. Mike's buggy down the road. "Thanks, Dr. Mike. But Myra needs to hear the words from your lips. I try to tell her the baby's fine, but Myra thinks I'm just praying out loud."

At the fork, Colleen stepped back and let Mr. Bing and Dr. Mike's buggy pass. She wasn't crazy about walking to school in the rain, but she knew how new Myra and Horace Bing were at being parents. Just about *everything* scared them to death. Colleen bit her lip, thinking that sometimes being a teenager was a little scary, too. Too bad she wasn't sick; then she'd be able to check into the clinic and talk privately to Dr. Mike.

When Colleen and Brian finally raced inside the schoolhouse, the rain was pounding like kettle drums against the tin roof. "I beat you!" laughed Brian.

"Guess you did, by three feet at least. Shake off your coat, Brian," suggested Colleen. "Let me see how wet your shoes are."

"Wet enough to squeak!"

"Put your shoes up by the stove, Brian. Give me your coat." Colleen pulled off her jacket and shook it before hanging it on one of the row of hooks. As she turned to get Brian's, she bumped into Blake Russell. "Sorry!"

"Whoa, looks like you swam to school, Colleen," Blake said. "Brian, come here, buddy. I think you might have a trout sticking out of your left ear."

Brian laughed and peeled off his coat. "Ma was gonna drive us, but she had to go help the Bings' baby stop hiccuping."

Blake raised an eyebrow. "There's only one *sure* way to stop the hiccups in Colorado Springs," said Blake. "You send Richard over. Legend has it, his face is guaranteed to scare the hiccups out of all people and *most* bears."

"Hardy-har!" said Richard. He swatted Blake on the arm. "Hey, speaking of scary, we can send *Colleen* over. Looks like she stuck her head in a bucket of something wet and green."

21

Colleen's hand flew up to her hair. "What?" She and Brian had taken a shortcut through the woods. What was in her hair?

"Richard's kidding." Blake's hand reached out and pulled Colleen's away. "You look okay."

Colleen nodded, then hurried past them to her seat. Alice was sitting on the corner of her desk, waiting.

"Well, you sure managed to make an entrance," said Alice. She glanced back at Blake, then frowned at Colleen. "Your mother is probably rolling in her grave at the way you've been throwing yourself at Blake Russell."

"What?" Colleen sank into her seat, glad to feel Becky's hand on her shoulder. "Be quiet about my mother. And . . ." Colleen clamped her mouth tight. Alice was very good at getting people so mad they flew off the handle.

Alice leaned down, her own hair glistening. "I see the way you follow him home after school. Won't be doing that too much longer, Colleen. Blake is coming home with *me* today."

"Go stand in the rain, Alice," mumbled Becky. "Talk to your friends, the worms."

Alice stood up. "Now, that's no way to win friends, Miss Becky Binder! You are hoping for at least a *few* votes today, aren't you?"

Becky stood up so fast, Colleen's schoolbooks slid off her desk. "We don't even want to be May

22

queen. So just go sharpen your horns someplace else, Alice!"

"Don't tell me what to do," snapped Alice. "And I know you want to be queen. Who wouldn't want to be queen?"

Colleen couldn't help but laugh. She was about to say that Dr. Mike, the most wonderful lady in town, didn't want to be a May queen, when she saw Reverend Johnson storming down the center aisle. Colleen wiped the smile off her face.

"Girls!" he cried, holding his piece of chalk high above his head. "What on earth is going on here?"

"Nothing!" all three girls said at once.

"Well, it was *something* loud enough to disrupt me from my preparations."

Colleen sat up straighter in her chair. "We . . . were just talking."

"Yes," agreed Alice. "About the May Day celebration. You are just the best teacher to allow us to experience English history, Reverend. By the way, my mother said she would be glad to help in any way. My pa said he would let you use his fancy buggy for a royal ride, and . . ."

Reverend held up both hands. "Thank you, Alice. Now, let me get back to work so we can start the nominations."

Alice waved her hand in Reverend's face. "I can save you some time with the nominations right now, Reverend. Colleen and Becky just told me

that they *positively* do not want to run for queen."
Alice smiled at the group of children who had
gathered to listen. "Of course, I would be honored
to take part in such a . . . a noble festival."

Reverend lowered his chalk. "What?"

"I said I would be *honored* to take part," Alice
began.

"Girls, what do you mean? You are refusing to
take part in the assignment?" Reverend did not
look a bit pleased.

"For once, Alice is right," admitted Becky.
"Colleen and I don't care about running for queen.
We would love to be Maypole dancers. We love
to dance."

Alice smiled. "I think that's a *great* idea."

"It's a *terrible* idea," cried Reverend. "This is
a school project, requiring every student's par-
ticipation. In England, the entire village partici-
pated."

"We want to participate, Reverend, as Maypole
dancers," replied Colleen.

"You see," cried Alice. "They *will* be part of it.
A *small* part, the part that doesn't involve being
queen." Alice nodded her head briskly. "It makes
perfect sense, Reverend. We need lots of dancers,
but only one queen. A queen who truly, truly
wants to be queen."

"You'd make a great *king*, Alice," said Richard.
"A tyrant!"

"Be quiet," Alice snapped.

"Students, we are missing the whole point of our festival. We are celebrating spring, the start of a new season and growth." Reverend Johnson set his chalk down on Colleen's desk and crossed his arms. "There is no such growth when people are refusing to participate fully. How can we have a fair, democratic election if almost half the possible queens in the upper section of the school refuse to run?"

Alice glanced around the room. "We can't *force* them to run, Reverend. And Missy still wants to run, and Laura, and . . . *me*, of course."

"As the teacher, I am a king of sorts," declared the Reverend. "And I decree that *all* girls twelve years and older, *if nominated*, will run for queen. Just like they did in England."

Colleen caught Blake's eye. He winked at her, and Colleen had to smile back. Wait until she told Dr. Mike about the full morning she had had. And school hadn't even started yet!

"I really love to dance," muttered Becky.

"Enough said," declared Reverend. He picked up his chalk and headed back to the front of the class. "Take your seats."

Colleen watched as Alice's face fell. "But, Reverend, this is Colorado Springs, Colorado, not London, England. I think we could bend a rule or two."

Reverend kept walking. "Every girl nominated will run. End of discussion."

Colleen and Becky sighed. Alice ground her back teeth.

Alice leaned down and scowled at them both. "Troublemakers! You'd better hope neither one of you gets nominated."

"Hey, Alice, your dragon is waiting outside for you," hooted Richard.

Alice turned so quickly that her damp curls brushed against Colleen's nose. "If I *had* a dragon, you'd be his lunch, Richard." With that, she marched off to her seat.

"Holy cow!" whispered Colleen. She'd read about kings and queens killing each other off to gain thrones in England. She sure hoped it was against the law in Colorado.

"I think we might be in a little bit of trouble," whispered Becky.

"Just ignore her," Colleen suggested. "I don't think we have to dig a moat around our seats for protection, yet."

Becky didn't smile back. Instead, she started to chew her thumbnail. "Well, maybe a little one. See, last night I saw Alice and her mother at Bray's store. I told Alice that you and I weren't going to run for queen."

Colleen nodded. "So?"

"So, Alice and her mother both got real excited,

and her mother sent all the way to Denver for material for her dress."

"Well, that's not our problem," Colleen said slowly.

"If Alice doesn't win, it might be," said Becky. She started biting off another fingernail.

Colleen smiled, for Becky's sake. "What are we worried about? Nobody is going to nominate us except each other. So I won't nominate you, and you won't nominate me." Colleen smiled when Becky grinned. "It's that simple."

A flash of lightning lit up a tree at the far corner of the playground. As the students raced to the windows, a boom of thunder rattled the tin roof. Seconds later, another flash of lightning sent many of the younger students back to their seats. A little girl in the front of the classroom started to cry. Colleen twisted in her seat to check on Brian. She caught his eye and smiled at him. He gave a small wave, and above his damp head, the blue eyes of Blake Russell stared straight back at Colleen.

As Colleen lowered her eyes, her heart began to pound with hammering blows. The schoolhouse windows rattled with the wind and the distant claps of thunder. Colleen drew in a deep breath and tried to steady her heart. She would have to talk to Dr. Mike about this. How could a simple look from Blake Russell cause such a reaction? Was it spring fever, like Dr. Mike said? Could spring fever cause your heart to pound as if a lion were chasing you? Or was the lion coming closer to investigate the pounding heart?

4

The sun broke through the gray clouds before lunch, causing the raindrops to glisten as they dangled from the branches outside the school. Inside the schoolhouse, the storm was just beginning. Every time Colleen looked up from her studies, Alice scowled at her. Every time Colleen looked in Blake's direction, he smiled at her.

"What's wrong? Colleen? You look like you've been into Dr. Mike's rouge pot," whispered Becky. "Do you feel all right?"

Colleen nodded, slowly drawing in a deep breath. She'd read about Cupid sneaking up and shooting his arrow into a person by surprise, but until now, she'd never believed it. Was she falling for Blake Russell? Was there some truth to the magic of spring?

"I'm . . . I'm okay," mumbled Colleen.

"Better ask Dr. Mike to mix you up a tonic," muttered Becky. "You look *terrible*."

Colleen nodded, trying not to smile. She felt *wonderful*.

Colleen was finishing her math sums when Alice walked past her desk, tossing a folded square paper into Colleen's lap. Becky made a face and shook her head. Colleen cupped her hand over the paper. Reverend had a very strict rule about note writing. You weren't allowed to do it! Colleen twisted quickly in her seat. Reverend Johnson was still working in the back of the room with two older students. Colleen glanced down at the note and bit her lip.

"Ohhhhh, that sneaky old Alice is just trying to get you in trouble," whispered Becky.

"Maybe she's writing to apologize."

"Ha! Fat chance of that!" snorted Becky. She slapped her hand over her mouth and slumped lower in her chair.

"Did you have a question, Becky?" asked Reverend Johnson.

Becky sat up straighter. "I . . . excuse me, but . . . I had something in my throat. Sorry." Becky coughed a few times, then smiled again. "I'm fine now, Reverend Johnson. Really."

Colleen bit her lip so she wouldn't smile. While Becky was coughing, she had carefully unfolded the note. As soon as she heard the Reverend explaining arithmetic once more, she glanced down at Alice's note. Becky frowned and leaned in closer to read.

DEAR COLLEEN,
I KNOW BUSY-BODY-BECKY IS
READING THIS. ONE DAY SHE
WILL HAVE HER OWN LIFE!!! YOU
TWO BETTER DO WHAT I SAY OR
THERE WILL BE TROUBLE. REV-
EREND JOHNSON DOES HAVE A
TEMPER! DO YOU WANT HIM TO
CANCEL MAY DAY? DOES THE
CROWN MEAN THAT MUCH TO
YOU? LEAVE THINGS TO ME. I
KNOW WHAT I'M DOING, WHICH IS
MORE THAN YOU CAN SAY!!!!!!!

Becky elbowed Colleen. "She doesn't know what she's doing!" Becky jabbed Colleen again. "I'm almost tempted to try and win, Colleen. Just to make sure Alice doesn't!"

Colleen nodded, covering Becky's mouth. "Hush, or we'll both get in trouble."

"A little late for that, ladies!"

Becky yelped! Colleen jumped in her seat as Reverend reached down and snatched the note. As he read, his eyebrows drew closer and closer together, his mouth remaining a firm, straight, disapproving line. Reverend finally low-ered the note. He closed his eyes and rubbed them.

"I know that looks like a note, Reverend," stam-mered Becky.

31

"It *is* a note, Becky." Reverend crossed his arms and waited.

"Yes, it is. But Colleen and I sure didn't write it. We just *read* it," Becky said in a rush. "It just landed on our desk."

Reverend Johnson began to tap his foot. Colleen concentrated on remaining calm.

"*Notes* do not just land, Becky. Someone delivered it. Someone who chose to *ignore* my rule about note writing, *and note reading*."

"Sorry, sir," mumbled Colleen. "I knew about the note-writing rule. Is the note-*reading* rule new?"

"No."

Colleen ducked her head.

"Sorry," added Becky. Becky picked up her pencil, tapping it against her paper. "And I'm sure the unfortunate girl who wrote the note that got Colleen and me in trouble is sorry, too."

Richard laughed. Reverend Johnson frowned.

"How do you know the unfortunate rule breaker is a girl?" Reverend Johnson studied the note. "There is no signature. Give me her name."

From behind Reverend's left shoulder, Colleen could see Alice shaking her head no, her hands clasped together as if in prayer.

Colleen cleared her throat. There was no way to get rid of the giant knot beginning to grow there. Becky tapped her pencil faster.

"Girls, I am waiting." Reverend Johnson let his

32

gaze touch all four corners of the schoolhouse. "Perhaps the author would like to stand up and declare herself."

The schoolhouse was quiet except for the crackling of wood in the stove.

"Perhaps this young lady is so weary from note writing that she needs a rest," continued Reverend. "Unless she stands quite quickly, she can take a *long* rest and excuse herself from taking part in the May Day festivities."

"But not us!" cried Becky. "Not the readers!"

Reverend shrugged. "Until the girl steps forward, you and Colleen are in as much trouble as she. Shielding a friend is admirable at times, but this is clearly not one of them. Perhaps you two shall have to shoulder the burden of . . ."

"Ask Alice what she knows," sputtered Becky.

"Be quiet, Becky," cried Alice. "I was just sitting here minding my own business."

"Girls!" Reverend boomed.

"Maybe we should let it pass, Reverend," suggested Blake. "You know, forgive our trespassers, and . . ."

Reverend turned around and studied Blake. He held the note high. "Don't make a joke of this, Blake. And don't take the Scriptures lightly."

Blake stood up. "I wasn't, Reverend. I was just repeating sound advice."

"Don't get involved, Mr. Russell," advised Reverend.

"I'm afraid I already *am*, sir." Blake paused, then took a deep breath. "I wrote the note."

The room was so still that Colleen could hear the logs crackling in the stove. She stared at her hands, the floor, anywhere but Blake's face.

"I had no idea note writing was such a crime," Blake went on. "I won't do it again, Reverend." Blake flashed his best smile at the class. "It isn't a hanging offense, is it, sir?"

Several boys laughed. Reverend Johnson held up his hand.

"There is little here that is a laughing matter. Note writing is not a major crime, of course. But it is against the rules of this school." Reverend folded the note and shoved it in his pocket. "I have very few rules to govern this school, so I will enforce those which I have created." Reverend Johnson looked down at Colleen. "Do you think that sounds fair, Colleen?"

"Yes, sir," she said quietly. She wasn't quite sure to what she had just agreed. Her head was beginning to pound.

"Some action will be taken," promised Reverend. He folded his arms and studied the class. His gaze went from Colleen back to Alice. He squinted, as if sensing there was a relationship, if only he could prove it.

"Sir?" Blake's low voice crackled against the silence. All heads turned and watched as he stood up and walked slowly toward the Reverend. "May

I speak to you privately?" Blake's face was solemn as he leaned forward and whispered into the Reverend's ear.

"What's that?" Reverend Johnson drew back, his own face erased of any emotion.

"I made a mistake, sir. A grave error in good judgment."

Alice was still staring down at her desk, but Colleen could see her hands trembling.

"It was meant to be a joke, Reverend," continued Blake. "I'm afraid I never heard the rule about note writing. Being new and all. I certainly wouldn't have violated such a firm rule. I beg your pardon, sir."

Reverend tapped the note against his hand. "I accept your apology, Mr. Russell. And I commend you for speaking to me when you did."

Colleen shook her head, her eyes still on Blake. Why was he doing this?

"I am still quite muddled about this incident," pondered Reverend. "Rules are rules, but as Shakespeare once said, 'A slave to rules is a king of tyrants . . .' "

Blake nodded, dropping his gaze to his feet. "My pa reads Shakespeare a lot. He thinks he was a real smart fella. My pa would probably feel bad about this, too. He would want me to help you out with some chores. To lighten your load a bit. You need wood cut for school. I'd be glad to volunteer."

Reverend nodded.

"Thank you, Reverend." Blake turned and walked slowly back to his seat.

Colleen forced herself to close her mouth. So many questions raced through her mind. Didn't Blake have a ma to answer to as well? Blake didn't write the note, so why was he lying? And most of all, why would he take the blame for someone as mean as Alice?

Within minutes, the classroom took on its normal, busy ticking. Reverend walked up and down the aisle, asking and answering questions. Students raised their hands, dropped their pencils, scribbled out wrong answers.

"Wow," muttered Becky. "I can't believe what I just witnessed. Colleen, explain to me, *what* is going on?"

Colleen shrugged, even though she thought she knew the answer. She swallowed quickly, feeling a tart bitterness travel down her throat and right into her heart. Her heart stung, then began a slow, unsure beating. There was only one reason Blake would take the blame for Alice O'Connor.

5

"**H**e does *not* like her," hissed Becky from behind her geography book.

"Yes, he does," Colleen whispered back. She put her finger to her lips to end the conversation. Colleen could barely concentrate on her studies. She couldn't understand what Blake liked about Alice. She was pretty, but not beautiful. She laughed a lot, but she never made any jokes herself. Colleen stared out the window, wondering if she would ever understand this spring fever business.

"Finish up your work and get your lunch pails," said Reverend.

"Reverend, my pa said he'll catch us a bear!" announced Caroline Beecher, a skinny little girl who sat in the front row. "Said he could catch one before Saturday."

Reverend smiled, then rubbed his forehead. "Thank you, Caroline. But what are we going to do with a bear?"

"Barbecue him!" hollered Richard from the back.

Caroline's neck flashed red, and she hunched down lower in her seat.

Reverend tugged on Caroline's braid. "Did you tell your pa about the bearbaiting, Caroline?"

"My pa liked that. I forgot some parts of the story."

Reverend smiled. "Well, in England, to celebrate May Day, some villages did chain a bear's leg or neck to a post and then tease him. I'm afraid the townsfolk in Colorado Springs might view this activity as a little too risky."

And mean, thought Colleen. Let the bear stay in his own world.

"Hey, Caroline, does your pa have a bear in mind, or maybe just one of his ugly relatives?" hooted Richard.

"Mind your manners, Mr. Petty," warned Reverend.

Caroline sank lower in her seat.

"Maybe we should tie Richard up!" joked Blake.

This time the whole class laughed. Colleen smiled as she watched Caroline turn and grin up at Blake. Blake had probably made the joke just to set the class laughing over something other than Caroline's pa.

A flicker of hope ignited inside Colleen. Maybe Blake didn't like Alice after all. He had a kind heart, which was why he always broke up fights on the playground and made sure everyone was included in yard games. Colleen smiled. Of course Blake would want to take the blame for Alice. The whole school knew how much she wanted to be in the May Day festival. Maybe Blake took the blame because he didn't care if he was in it or not.

Colleen shook her head, glad she was finally beginning to understand. Colleen answered the last two geography questions and handed in her paper. On the way back to her seat, she smiled at Blake. She felt so happy all of a sudden, she smiled at Alice, too.

Five minutes later, when Reverend rang the lunch bell, Colleen was starving. She grabbed Becky, and the two of them raced out of the schoolhouse.

"Well, you certainly are in a good mood," said Becky. She brushed off the wooden bench and sat down. "Let's share."

"Okay." Colleen handed over a ham-and-cheese biscuit and took Becky's hard-boiled egg. Colleen took a bite and nodded. "This is good."

Becky giggled. "You are burning up with spring fever, Colleen. I could have given you a wood chip and you'd be raving about it right now."

"Only a barbecued wood chip," laughed Colleen. She picked up her water jar and took a long sip. Through the clear glass, she could see Blake and Brian sitting under the tree. "Brian thinks Blake is the nicest boy in the world."

"So it runs in the family, huh?" said Becky.

"I am not sweet on him," insisted Colleen. "But he is my friend."

"Of course he is," Becky agreed. "And that's why you practically dropped dead an hour ago when you thought he liked Alice."

"I was confused, that's all." Colleen unwrapped a biscuit. "But now I know that Blake was just being Blake. He comes to the rescue of anyone in trouble."

Becky stood up. "Where's the nearest quick-sand pit?"

"What?"

Becky sat down again. "I want to jump in so Blake can rescue me."

"Oh, you." Colleen grinned at her friend. "Let's eat fast and go over and watch the boys carve."

"Watch all the boys, or just one boy?" questioned Becky.

Colleen shrugged. "I'm going over to watch Brian. He's still a little young to be working with such a big knife."

"Does Dr. Mike know?"

Colleen shook her head. "No, part of it is a surprise. Blake is showing Brian how to carve a hook, so she can hang up her stethoscope at the clinic."

"Just what she doesn't want," giggled Becky.

"Ma loves anything Brian makes."

Becky set her biscuit down. "Colleen, does it still feel funny? Having Dr. Mike, and not having your ma?"

Colleen's eyes stung. Even though Becky was her best friend, she didn't like to talk about her mother's death with anyone. No one except Dr. Mike.

"You don't have to answer, sorry," Becky said quickly.

Colleen picked up her water jar. "Thanks."

Before the girls had time to pack up their lunches, Blake and Brian walked over and sat down with them.

"Look, Colleen," cried Brian. He held out an oddly shaped wooden J. "It's a hook for Ma's clinic."

Colleen took the hook and turned it over. "You did a great job, Brian. Is it finished?"

Brian's face fell.

Blake took the hook from Colleen and held it up. "Your sister means, are you going to add a coat of varnish, or paint it?"

Brian studied Colleen's face. "You like it, Colleen? Will Ma like it in her May basket?"

"She will love it, Brian," Colleen said. She smiled at Blake, thankful for yet another rescue. "What will it be? Painting or varnish?"

"Sully has some red paint left from the barn," said Brian.

41

"And Ma loves just plain white," added Colleen.

Brian grinned. "Maybe both, like a peppermint hook."

"Go set the hook next to my knife, Brian," said Blake. "But don't let anyone but Richard use my knife."

"Okay!" Brian raced across the playground, his hook now a bird soaring up and down beside him.

Becky handed Blake a cookie. "Boy, all you need is a suit of armor and you'd be Colorado's own King Arthur."

"Or our very own Robin Hood," said Colleen. "You are very good at helping people out of sticky situations, Blake."

Blake stood up and bowed. "At your service, ladies."

"You'd make a great king," said Becky. "Want to be one?"

"Becky!" Colleen's own cheeks felt warm. It was hard to remember the shy Becky who sat under this very tree last year.

"I guess I'd be interested in being king if the right girl ended up as queen," teased Blake.

Becky laughed. "Well, old Alice is trying her hardest to get every kid's vote. Has she offered you a horse if you'd vote for her?"

Blake smiled and shook his head. "No."

Colleen set her water jar down and tried to keep her voice steady. "Why did you take the blame for writing the note, Blake?"

"I had my reasons," Blake said. He grinned at Colleen. "Maybe I didn't want *you* getting kicked out of May Day. Reverend's neck was getting red, and he was ready to pounce on someone. You were right beside him, Colleen."

Colleen smiled. "Thanks. I thought maybe you . . ."

Becky leaned forward. "The truth is, Colleen and I thought you did it 'cause you were sweet on Alice."

Blake looked surprised. "Oh, well . . ."

"Well, *are* you?" asked Becky. "I mean, as long as the subject is up."

Colleen sighed. Becky was unbelievable!

Blake reached down and grabbed another cookie from Becky's pail. "No, I'm not sweet on Alice. See you girls later."

As soon as his words were out, Colleen started to smile. She forced herself to keep her head down as Blake walked away, but she couldn't control the flood of happiness rushing around inside. Blake *didn't* like Alice!

"See," Becky went on, chewing her cookie and waving her hand. "All you have to do is communicate with people, Colleen. People drive each other crazy and no one wants to admit it. People have questions, but they're afraid to ask for the answers. That's the problem with the world."

Colleen nodded, suddenly famished. She

reached into Becky's pail and got out a cookie. She had opened her mouth to take a bite when Becky grabbed her wrist and squeezed.

"Hey, I only took one," cried Colleen.

"Look at that!"

Colleen looked up and her heart nearly flew out of her mouth. Alice was circling Blake as if he were a raccoon about to be treed. She was shaking her head back and forth so fast, her hair ribbons untangled and fell to the ground. Within seconds, Alice had scooped up her ribbons and was dragging Blake by the hand toward the shadowy blue spruce grove the little children used for hide-and-go-seek.

"Look at her go!" muttered Becky. "If we could only find a way to hitch a plow to her, she could till an acre before sundown."

Colleen watched as Blake's red shirt disappeared behind a blue spruce.

Colleen watched the grove, waiting for Blake to reappear. How long would it take him to tell Alice to please leave him alone? Two minutes passed. A third minute.

Five minutes later, Colleen stood up so fast that her orange rolled across the grass. Leaving her lunch pail behind, Colleen hurried toward the schoolhouse.

"Colleen, wait up!" called Becky.

Colleen wanted to wait, but she was too mad to stop. Mad at Blake for all the dumb games he

played. Mad at herself for believing him. By the
time Colleen hurried up the steps, she had come
to a decision. Blake could continue with his games;
he was very good at them. But from now on, Colleen Cooper wasn't playing.

6

"**N**ice of you both to join us," Reverend Johnson said as Blake and Alice hurried into the schoolroom.

Colleen kept her eyes straight ahead, reminding herself that Blake and Alice were of no interest to her at all. They were just another game, like bobbing for apples or a taffy pull. Colleen sat up straighter, feeling very proud of herself for her decision to ignore Blake Russell for the rest of her life.

"All right now, class," Reverend Johnson began. "Let's have our nominations for May queen and king. Then we can pick the six Morris dancers." Reverend rubbed his hands together. "This is going to be such fun. There will be ten to twelve Maypole dancers as well. Mr. Bray has ordered in a fine collection of ribbon streamers."

Becky grabbed Colleen's hand and squeezed it. "It will be so much fun to be May dancers together! Has Dr. Mike started working on your dress yet?"

Colleen shook her head. Lately, Dr. Mike returned from the clinic so tired that Colleen didn't have the heart to ask her for another thing. Who cared about a dumb dress now, anyway?

"Nominations for queen first." Reverend tapped the chalk against his fingertips. "Now, who will get things going for us?"

Alice's *ladies-in-waiting*, Susie and Patricia, waved their arms back and forth.

"Reverend, oh, Reverend!" cried Patricia.

"Yes, Patricia?"

"Reverend, I nominate Alice. I'm sure the whole class would agree that she would make a great queen."

Colleen watched as Alice tried to look surprised.

"Thank . . . you, Patricia," stammered Alice. She halfway stood up and smiled at everyone. "I'd be honored. And my mother has a silver crown if we need it."

Two little girls in the front of the room clapped.

"I'd like to second that nomination," added Susie Wilson. "And I'd like to nominate Patricia and myself for Maypole dancers. Our mothers will help decorate, too. Plus, our mothers have offered to donate six dozen fudge squares."

"But will they chop wood?" Richard called out.

Reverend frowned at Richard. "It is a shame none of this creativity finds its way into your lessons, Mr. Petty." Reverend turned and printed Alice's name on the board under the title of QUEEN, and Susie and Patricia under DANCERS. "Let's have some more nominations, class."

"I nominate Colleen!" Brian called out. "She's the best sister in the whole world!"

The class laughed. Colleen turned and smiled at her little brother. He had no idea how embarrassing this was.

"Of course you may," said Reverend.

"I second the nomination," said Becky quickly.

"I *question* the nomination!" Richard called out from the back of the room.

"Oh, go soak your head, Richard Petty!" snapped Becky.

"Thanks," whispered Colleen. She looked up and met Alice's eyes. Alice gave a very fake smile and turned around so quickly that her curls knocked against Patricia's head.

"Richard, you seem to want to take part in the festivities," Reverend commented. "Let's direct your energy into something more constructive. I'm going to put you in charge of the Morris dancers and skits."

"What?" squeaked Richard. He sat up straighter in his seat. "I was only joking, Colleen. She knew that, didn't you, Colleen? I mean, hey, I'll even vote for you!"

"You said you would vote for *me*!" cried Alice.

Reverend nodded his head and turned to write Richard's name under MORRIS SKIT. "You will be in charge of picking five dancers, Richard. The sixth dancer will be the queen of the May, and we won't know who she is until the morning of the celebration."

"But, Reverend," Alice blurted out. "How will the queen have time to practice her part for the skit? I won't . . . I mean, the *queen* won't have time to learn her lines."

Becky jabbed Colleen. "Alice thinks she's already wearing the crown."

"Very good point, Alice." Reverend rubbed his chin. "Perhaps all the girls nominated for queen could memorize the part. Richard, when you write the skit, distribute a copy to each girl nominated."

"You mean I have to make up a little play all by myself? And . . . and how do I make copies?"

Blake turned around and grinned at Richard. "You write one part over and over again, Richard. Kind of like you're *copying* it."

Colleen listened as Reverend and the rest of the class laughed. She sat up straighter, frowned, and drew in a deep breath. Blake thought he was so funny.

"Blake, you have a fine sense of humor," Reverend commented.

"Thank you, sir."

"Why don't we put that sense of humor to best

advantage and have you help Richard with the Morris skit?" suggested Reverend.

Richard let out a sigh and leaned back in his seat. "Blake can have the job if he wants, Reverend."

Reverend shook his head. "Things will go much more smoothly if you two work together."

Reverend turned and walked back to the blackboard. "Now, do I have any more nominations?"

Colleen barely listened as more and more names were added to the chalkboard. Colleen was in the running for queen, and Becky was going to be a Maypole dancer. At least *one* of them would have a good time at the festival.

"I wish you could be a Maypole dancer," whispered Becky. "But I'll bet you win for queen."

Colleen tried to smile. It didn't matter anymore. Why bother to celebrate spring? All of a sudden, it didn't seem so special.

7

By the time school was dismissed, Colleen had a splitting headache. She was dreading the walk home with Becky, who would want to talk about Blake and Alice the entire trip.

"Hey, there's my mother!" said Becky as the two girls left the school.

Colleen felt relieved to see Becky's mother waiting at the end of the school lane with a buggy.

"Come along, Becky dear," called out Mrs. Binder. "We need to get some ribbon for your festival dress."

Becky's eyes brightened. "Colleen, do you want to come? Maybe Dr. Mike could leave the clinic for a half hour and pick out some ribbons for *your* dress."

Colleen shook her head. "I don't even have a dress, Becky. Thanks, anyway. I'd better get home and start supper."

"Okay, but if you want to wear something of mine, let me know," called Becky as she raced to the buggy. "Remind Dr. Mike that we only have *three* more days till the festival."

Colleen watched as Mrs. Binder hugged her daughter and the two of them drove off toward Loren Bray's general store. Both of them were talking a mile a minute. Colleen shifted her book strap. Maybe she should walk into town and see if Dr. Mike needed any help at the clinic. It would be like old times. Maybe with an extra hand, Dr. Mike would be able to leave early, and the two of them could drive home together.

Colleen looked around the schoolyard for Brian. She would ask him to go straight home and start his chores. Then, after supper, she would offer to help him paint the hook for Dr. Mike.

Colleen cupped her hands and called, "Brian! Brian!"

"Brian left already."

Colleen spun around. Blake was coming from around the side of the schoolhouse, carrying an ax.

"Brian already left?" questioned Colleen.

"He left with Richard and Paul," said Blake.

"What was he doing with the older boys?" asked Colleen.

Blake lowered the ax. "Richard said he'd give Brian a square of sanding paper. To use on the hook for Dr. Mike."

Colleen swung her book strap over her left shoulder. The afternoon sun was blazing after the morning shower. "He should have told me."

Blake nodded. "He was pretty excited about getting the present ready for Dr. Mike."

Colleen turned to leave.

"If you wait another five minutes, I'll walk you home," Blake offered.

Colleen shook her head. "No thanks. You seem busy enough."

Colleen heard the thwack of the ax biting into the wood.

"Colleen!"

Colleen stopped and turned around. "What?"

"Tell Brian to bring my knife back tomorrow."

"What?" Colleen hurried back to the woodpile. "You gave your knife to my little brother?"

"Brian was holding it for me. I forgot to get it back."

Colleen couldn't believe her ears. "So my little brother, who isn't even allowed to *have* a knife, is walking around with yours?"

"What are you talking about?"

"Brian is not allowed to use a knife yet. Dr. Mike said no to him when he asked."

Blake shot Colleen a confused look. "So, if he wasn't allowed to use it, why did you let him use mine?"

"Because I trusted you!" sputtered Colleen. "Because he was making Dr. Mike a surprise and . . ." Colleen heard the shaking in her own voice and stopped. "I made a mistake."

Blake's face softened. "He's okay. I told him not to take it out of the holder. I'll get it back tomorrow."

Colleen nodded. "Thank you." She turned and started to walk away again.

"Why'd you use past tense?"

Colleen stopped, but didn't turn. "What?"

"You said you *trusted* me." Blake sent another slice of the ax through the wood.

"Nothing," Colleen said. "Never mind."

Blake held the ax for a second, then shattered the rest of the log in three whacks with the ax. "Just curious."

Colleen turned, using every bit of concentration to keep the anger out of her voice. "You don't always tell the truth, Blake."

"What?" Blake looked more hurt than angry.

"I know . . ." Colleen stopped. Why had she opened her mouth?

"You know what?" Blake dropped the ax and took a step closer to Colleen. "Did somebody tell you something about me?"

"No. Besides, it's none of my business," Colleen said quickly. "It just shocked me, that's all."

"Seems like you made it yours," snapped Blake. "No matter how many towns we move to, someone has to go digging up dirt." Blake waved her away with his hand. "Go on. I don't care anymore. Listen to what you want. Believe what you want."

Colleen had never seen Blake angry before, but he was angry now. She wanted to say that she didn't trust him anymore because he lied about liking Alice. His face was set hard. Now didn't seem like a good time to talk. Besides, Blake and Alice weren't any of her business.

Colleen decided against going to the clinic. She wanted to get home as soon as possible and get the knife away from Brian. She hurried up the lane, pushing up the sleeves of her sweater. She was about to duck under Mr. Harris's fence and take the shortcut when she spotted Alice, Susie, and Patricia clustered in a tight circle. Alice was talking at top speed.

Colleen froze. Susie looked up and spied her. "We have a visitor!"

"Hi," Colleen said. She decided against the shortcut. She didn't want them thinking she was avoiding them. She kept on walking.

Alice put her hand on her hip. "Well, aren't you in a big hurry? Where's your shadow, Becky?"

"Her mother picked her up," said Colleen.

Alice looked disappointed as Colleen walked past her. "I just hope you didn't hear anything *private* when you snuck up on us."

"Yeah," agreed Patricia. "If we had known our discussion wasn't going to be confidential, we would have gone someplace else."

Colleen bit the inside of her lip so she wouldn't

be tempted to say anything back. It was a good thing Becky wasn't with her. Becky had a very short fuse.

"Let her go, girls," said Alice. "Colleen wouldn't be interested in my *big* news."

"It's *very* big news," added Patricia. "Alice just told us all about it."

Colleen hoped it was *good* news, like Alice and her family moving out of Colorado Springs.

From behind her, Colleen could hear Alice laughing. "Yes, hurry and find your brother, Colleen. Better thank him for nominating you. I guess I'm lucky I didn't have to bribe a relative."

Colleen wasn't sure if her splitting headache made her turn around, or her own short fuse. "First of all, I *didn't* bribe him, Alice," insisted Colleen. "And secondly . . ."

"Oh, sure," Alice broke in. "Like you didn't offer him a penny bag of candy."

"No, that's what *you've* been offering for votes," Colleen pointed out. "I hope Mr. Bray has enough peppermint sticks in stock to cover your bribes."

"I'm not bribing little kids to vote for me," cried Alice. "What kind of weasel would offer a peppermint stick for a vote?"

"Yeah," interrupted Susie, taking a big step closer to Colleen. "We're offering a *nickel's* worth of *gumdrops!*"

"Susie!" snapped Alice.

"What?" cried Susie. "It's a good deal!"

56

Colleen laughed. The entire May Day festival was turning into a circus.

"Susie! Why'd you tell?" demanded Alice. "Boy, can't you keep a secret?"

"Sure I can, Alice," whined Susie. "I just didn't want her thinkin' you were cheap, that's all."

"You are so *dumb*," continued Alice. "Come on, Patricia. Susie, go learn how to keep your mouth shut."

"I didn't tell her about the grove!" cried Susie.

Alice turned and clamped her hand over Susie's mouth. "Don't you dare say another word!" Alice picked up her book strap and marched quickly away.

Colleen watched Susie scurrying along behind, apologizing and trying to keep up.

I already know about the grove! Colleen wanted to shout. And I don't care.

With each heavy step, Colleen told herself again and again that she didn't care. By the time she reached the fork in the road, she halfway believed it.

8

Colleen found Brian busy with his chores in the barn.

"Hi, Brian."

Brian added another cup of oats to Taffy's trough. "Want to go riding with me, Colleen?"

"No, thanks. I have to start supper." Colleen walked over to Brian's stack of schoolbooks. "Want me to take these into the house for you?"

Brian nodded. "Thanks. Not the sanding paper, though. I want to keep it out here so Ma won't see the hook."

"Can I take Blake's knife inside?"

Brian shook his head. "Nah. He said I was big enough to hold it for him."

"But don't use it, Brian. You know how Dr. Mike feels about knives."

"I am big enough," insisted Brian. "Matthew had his own knife when he was my age."

"Maybe Sully will get you one for Christmas."

"I'm big enough now," Brian repeated. "I'm the

only boy at school who doesn't have one."

"Don't worry Ma about it, Brian," said Colleen. "She's real tired right now."

"I know." Brian picked up a brush and began to comb Taffy's mane. "That's why I'm only complaining to you. Sully told me to leave Ma be."

"Be sure you give Blake his knife back first thing in the morning, Brian." Colleen bent down and picked up his books. "And if you take Taffy out for a ride, leave the knife here."

"You sound just like Ma," laughed Brian. He pulled the large knife in its leather holder from his pocket and laid it on the barn chest. "I'll keep it here, okay?"

Colleen smiled. "Okay. And Brian?"

"What?"

"Thanks for nominating me for May queen today."

"You're welcome." Brian walked to the side of his horse, rubbing his hand up and down her coat. "Blake told me to do it."

"What?" Colleen leaned against the side of the barn door. "When did he tell you that?"

Brian squinted one eye shut as he tried to think. "He told me to last week, and then he told me to on Monday, and then he whispered it to me when we got to school this morning."

"Why would he do that?"

"He likes you."

"Me and the rest of the girls at school," muttered Colleen. "Keep track of time, Brian. I'm going in to start supper."

Colleen was glad to busy herself with supper preparations. It kept her mind occupied. By the time the stew was bubbling, Sully was washing up outside, and Dr. Mike rode up on horseback. Colleen pulled the biscuits from the oven, smiling as she listened to Sully and Dr. Mike laughing. Maybe things at the clinic were lightening up. Colleen set the biscuits inside a towel and peeked outside. Brian and Taffy had just arrived at the barn as well.

"Hurry and wash up, Brian," called Sully.

Brian raced up from the barn, and all three of them bustled in through the front door together.

"It smells wonderful, Colleen," Sully said.

Dr. Mike nodded. "I didn't have time to stop for lunch, so I hope you made a lot, Colleen."

"I'm starving," announced Brian. "I brushed Taffy and cleaned out her stall, Sully. Nobody even had to ask me."

"I'm proud of you, son," said Sully.

Colleen set the basket of biscuits on the table, then grabbed a towel and picked up the heavy black pot of stew. "Brian, get the pitcher of water, please."

Dr. Mike sank into her chair. "It feels good to sit down. Three more patients came in today. But I think two are going home tomorrow. I'm wondering if there is an end to the line."

"Make sure they all go home by Saturday, Ma," said Brian. "Blake said he might give me a part in his skit, and I want you and Sully to watch me."

"I hope things have calmed down by then," said Dr. Mike. She yawned and then smiled. "Let's have our blessing before Colleen's good food gets cold."

Colleen silently added her own prayer when the blessing was finished. Dear God, she prayed. Keep me from judging people so quickly. Remind me that Blake and Alice are your children, too.

"You asleep, Colleen?" asked Brian.

Colleen's eyes flew open. "No."

"Boy, school was sure fun today!" Brian announced. He held his plate up for stew. "First of all, I got to get soaking wet, and then Reverend yelled at Colleen."

"Brian!" Colleen gave him a small kick under the table.

"What?" Dr. Mike looked at Colleen. "What happened?"

"Reverend didn't yell. Not much, anyway."

Brian picked up a biscuit. "Yeah. Mostly Reverend yelled in a low, sad voice. Right, Colleen? That voice he uses when we break his rules and stuff."

"Exactly which rules did you break, Colleen?" Dr. Mike set her fork down and waited.

Colleen shrugged. "Someone passed me a note. That's all. I just opened it, and then Reverend came over and took it."

Brian laughed. "Then Blake told Reverend *he* wrote it." Brian laughed again.

"What's so funny about that?" Dr. Mike wondered. "I don't think rules should be broken."

"Blake *didn't* write the note," explained Brian. "Alice wrote the note." Brian leaned forward on his elbows. "I saw her do it."

"But Blake told Reverend he wrote it," said Dr. Mike.

Colleen studied Dr. Mike a second before nodding. It would be so embarrassing if Dr. Mike went to the school and told Reverend the truth. It would just be upsetting the whole applecart again. Alice would deny it, anyway.

"Why did Blake take the blame?" asked Sully. "I don't understand."

Colleen nearly choked on her stew. Trying to explain why Blake Russell did anything would take a week of Sundays.

Dr. Mike yawned. "Excuse me." She glanced down at her plate. "I guess my eyes were bigger than my stomach. I'm not very hungry after all."

"Do you feel okay, Dr. Mike?" asked Colleen.

Dr. Mike reached over and patted Colleen's hand. "Your biscuits are as light as ever. I'm just tired."

Colleen glanced at Dr. Mike's plate. She hadn't eaten more than a forkful.

Dr. Mike got up from her chair and went to the stove for the coffeepot. "So, tell me more about your day at school, children."

"I nominated Colleen to be the queen," announced Brian.

Sully smiled at Colleen. "Prettiest girl nominated, I'm sure."

"Alice will win," mumbled Brian from behind his biscuit.

"Brian!" Dr. Mike handed Sully a cup of coffee and sat down with her own. "Colleen has just as good a chance of winning as Alice O'Connor does."

"Not really," admitted Brian. "Alice said she would give me two bags of candy if I voted for her."

Colleen groaned. "Well, you might as well take the candy, Brian. I'm not going to win." Colleen pushed away her own plate. "I don't even want to go to the festival."

"The festival is Saturday!" Dr. Mike put her hand on her cheek. "Colleen, we have to do something about your dress."

"I can wear my red one," said Colleen.

"No, that's much too warm for spring." Dr. Mike stood up quickly. "I'll check my trunk. I'm sure I . . ."

Dr. Mike held onto the back of her chair. Sully hopped up from his seat and put his arms around her shoulders. "Are you all right?"

Dr. Mike rubbed her forehead. "I just got a little light-headed for a second. Maybe I need some fresh air."

"You need to relax," said Sully. "Come on. Let's sit outside."

"Do you want some water, Ma?" asked Colleen. She opened the front door.

Dr. Mike shook her head. "No. Really, I feel fine now."

Colleen closed the door softly behind Sully and Dr. Mike. Dr. Mike didn't look fine. She looked exhausted.

"Is Ma okay?" Brian looked scared.

"Sure," Colleen said quickly. "She's been working hard, that's all. Finish up now and then start your lessons. We don't want to worry Dr. Mike about a single thing."

Brian nodded. "I won't tell her about the knife."

Colleen spun around. "Especially don't tell her about the knife. And give it back to Blake as soon as you see him."

"Okay." Brian took a bite of biscuit, then set it back down. "Ma won't die, will she, Colleen?"

Colleen slid onto the bench beside him and put her hand on the back of his neck. "Ma isn't sick, Brian. She's just tired."

"Promise?"

Colleen nodded. "She's very healthy. Don't you worry."

Brian picked up his biscuit and added a spoonful of jam.

Colleen cleared the table, wrapping Dr. Mike's plate and setting it on the stove. "Do you want any cake, Brian?"

When he didn't answer, Colleen turned and found him poking at his palm with his fork. "What are you doing?"

Brian grimaced. "I have a big splinter. But I don't want to bother Ma, since she's tired."

"Let me see." Colleen took his hand and held it closer to the window. "That looks deep, Brian. When did you get this?"

Brian ducked his head. "Today. In the grove."

"The grove?" Colleen dropped his hand. "When?"

"At lunch." Brian rubbed his palm. "Don't tell Blake though. I wasn't spying."

"Were you in the grove when Blake and Alice were there?"

"I wasn't spying," Brian said softly. "I was already up in a tree, and then they came running in."

"You were there first. You weren't spying, Brian."

Brian looked relieved. "I know. And I had to keep my eyes open, didn't I? Otherwise, I'd fall right out of the tree."

Colleen studied her own palm. "So, did you hear what they talked about?"

Brian shook his head. "No. Alice was jabbering away, and then Blake started to leave."

Colleen smiled. "He did? So, he didn't want to stand there talking to Alice?"

Brian shook his head again. "He wanted to leave, all right. He should have run right out of there."

"Why, was Alice being mean?"

"No."

Colleen dipped a napkin in water and rubbed Brian's palm. "This splinter doesn't look too bad. I'll get Ma's bag and pull it right out, Brian."

"Thanks. And then we don't have to let Blake know I saw him in the grove."

"He won't care." Colleen laughed. "Everyone knows how Alice is." Colleen reached for the bag, wondering if she owed Blake an apology. It wasn't his fault Alice followed him around like a puppy dog. Blake's problem was that he was too nice to everyone.

"But don't tell Blake I was there," repeated Brian. He held out his palm to Colleen. "He might get all red-faced."

"Why?"

" 'Cause then he would know."

Colleen gave an exasperated sigh. "Brian, stop talking in riddles. Blake will not care that you saw him in the grove with Alice. I saw him walk into the grove, too. So did Becky. So did lots of kids."

Brian winced as Colleen jabbed at the splinter. "Yeah," he said softly. "But I was the only one who saw Blake kiss Alice."

Colleen paused, then pulled the thin splinter out.

"Ouch," cried Brian, pulling away. "That hurts!"

"I know," Colleen said softly. "It hurts a lot."

9

"Feeling better, Michaela?" Sully wrapped his arms more tightly around her.

She nodded. "I hope I didn't worry the children." She leaned back against Sully, looking up at the stars. "When am I going to find time to get Colleen ready for the festival?"

"She's a big girl. I expect she can find a dress."

Michaela sighed. "I *want* to help her. A girl needs another woman's advice. Lately, the only advice I'm giving is how to get rid of the grippe."

Sully gave a deep laugh and tightened his arms around Michaela's waist. "I'll help Colleen with the dress."

Michaela smiled. "You'll have her wearing rabbit fur in May. Thanks, but I am going to have to find the time. Being fourteen seems a lot more complicated for girls than for boys, Sully."

"Are you sure you feel all right now?"

Michaela nodded. "I feel fine."

"Good," he said, pulling her to her feet. "Because I want to show you something."

Dr. Mike glanced back at the house. "Brian already said good night. Should I check on Colleen?"

Sully shook his head. "No need. She already went to her room. Besides, this won't take but a minute. We'll still be within callin' distance if Colleen comes out on the porch lookin' for us."

"I worry about Colleen. She works so hard."

"We all do," Sully pointed out.

"But you're only young once."

Sully put his arm around Michaela's shoulders. "Come on and take a walk with me. I've been saving this surprise for a long time."

Michaela leaned closer against him. "I love surprises."

"I love you," whispered Sully, kissing her head.

Michaela felt stronger with each step. Her days were long and filled with a thousand duties, but coming home to Sully and the children made everything worthwhile.

"Close your eyes," said Sully. He took her by the hand and carefully led her between two huge pine trees. He brought her to the edge of a clearing and kissed her cheek. "Okay, you can open them now."

Michaela opened her eyes on a small, beautiful pond, banked with freshly turned earth. A small tree held a tiny birdhouse, and a long, narrow bench faced the pond.

"Oh, Sully. It's lovely!" Michaela walked over

and sat down on the bench. She ran her hand along the smooth wood. "You made this for me?"

"You can come here to relax. It's not as fancy as the garden behind your mother's house in Boston, but once we get some seeds planted, and maybe a cherry tree or two, it will look fine."

"You remembered how much I loved reading by my father's pond," Michaela said softly. She looked up at Sully, tears glistening in her eyes. "Thank you."

Sully sat on the bench next to her. "Promise me you'll come here and rest more."

Michaela reached for his hand. "Promise me you'll always love me this much."

Sully kissed her fingertips. "I promise."

Suddenly, Dr. Mike stood up. "Did you hear something? Was that Colleen?"

Sully reached up and pulled her back down. "No, not unless she's turned into a screech owl. Sit down and tell me what kind of seeds you want Loren to order. We better send out for them tomorrow."

Dr. Mike nodded, but kept turning her head. "I really think I hear her. Maybe she wants to talk. Used to be, I would have to ask her to slow down with her stories. First time I ever met Colleen, she was following her mother around talking a mile a minute. She's been quiet lately. Wish I knew why."

"Children get quieter as they grow."

Dr. Mike grinned. "Is that a medical fact?"

Sully stopped, turning her face toward him. "I love you, that's a fact. Now, don't invent a problem on such a perfect night." Sully pointed up. "Look, a falling star. Make a wish."

Dr. Mike watched as the blazing light fell slowly down across the dark sky.

Michaela leaned her head against his chest. She closed her eyes, feeling safe, tired, happy. When she opened them again, Sully was carrying her up the steps to the front porch.

"I fell asleep," she whispered.

"I decided not to leave you down by the pond," chuckled Sully.

"Thanks." Michaela yawned, looking over Sully's shoulder at the twinkling stars blazing brightly against the black night. "I forgot to make a wish," she said. "I forgot all about wishing on that falling star."

"I made one for you," whispered Sully, quietly opening the door and stepping inside.

Dr. Mike smiled, ready to ask him about the wish, but she had already fallen back to sleep.

10

Early the next morning, Colleen was awakened by a gentle breeze billowing the lace curtains across her pillow. The soft brushing against her cheek felt so gentle, pulling her slowly from her dreams. She sat up, stretching, happy to see such a beautiful sunrise beyond the lace panels.

"Today is a new day," Colleen whispered. "I want it to be filled with good thoughts, and good deeds. I'm not going to let anyone ruin it for me." She flopped back against her pillows. Blake Russell was driving her crazy. Why couldn't she stop thinking about him? The way she was feeling went far beyond a simple case of spring fever. Colleen sat up in bed and sighed. If only she could race into Dr. Mike's room and talk to her. Dr. Mike was as wise and understanding as Colleen's real ma had been. But Dr. Mike was also part friend, part older sister.

Colleen kicked away the sheets and climbed out

of bed. Once she was awake, her thoughts raced through her mind too quickly to fall back to sleep. Colleen grabbed her robe and tiptoed to her washstand. Once the cold water hit her face, she would be able to start deciding about her day. Colleen shook her head. Lately, her decisions went back and forth, racing up and down like the jutting outline of the Rockies.

Colleen rolled the bar of soap around and around before lathering up her face. Washing one's face each morning and each night was such an ordinary task. If only a day's mistakes could be splashed away at night, a morning's dreams lathered on each morning.

Colleen met her eyes in the mirror and grinned. No matter what happened, she refused to fall into the pit of foaming madness that surrounded spring. Other people might act unusual at this time of year, but Colleen Cooper was determined to stay exactly the same. There had to be a sensible reason why being thirteen had been an easier year than this. It couldn't possibly be that living in Colorado Springs had been simpler before Blake Russell moved to town.

"He's just a boy!" Colleen muttered to herself from behind her towel. She wiped her face clean and hung the towel on the brass hook by the window. Once again, Colleen looked out at the pink and faded gray sky.

The night before, Colleen had had a hard time

falling asleep, tossing and getting tangled in her bedsheets, wondering what really happened between Blake and Alice. Had Brian been able to see clearly from his treetop view? At almost eleven o'clock, when Colleen slipped out of bed to get a drink of water, she got her journal out and started to write.

DEAR DIARY,
AM I GLAD BRIAN TOLD ME ABOUT BLAKE KISSING ALICE. IN MY HEART, I KNEW HE KISSED HER. WHY ELSE WERE THEY IN THE GROVE? I AM SURE THEY WERE NOT PLAYING HIDE-AND-GO-SEEK. THE MAIN THING IS, EVEN THOUGH BLAKE IS THE MOST HANDSOME, AND THE KINDEST BOY I HAVE EVER MET, I DO NOT KNOW HIM. I MUST NOT KNOW HIM IF HE LIKES ALICE ENOUGH TO KISS HER. NOT EVERYONE WHO LOOKS PERFECT ON THE OUTSIDE IS PERFECT ON THE INSIDE. THAT SOUNDS DUMB, BUT MAYBE IT'S PRETTY SMART. OH, WHO CARES ANYWAY. I JUST WANT TO LIKE WAKING UP AND HAVING A NICE DAY.

Colleen wiped the last bit of sleep from her eyes. Today was another chance for a fresh start. And she wouldn't be wasting it by meddling in Blake's love life. She had her own life to live. Colleen grabbed her school dress from the hook and stepped into her stockings and shoes.

"Let the sun shine in." Colleen laughed as she pushed back her lace curtains and pulled up her bed quilt. She buttoned her cuffs as she hurried into the kitchen. The stove was already lit, with the black kettle simmering on the back burner. Colleen smiled, peeking from the front window to watch Sully walking slowly into the barn.

Sully was yawning and stretching, but seemed glad to be awake and part of the new day. Colleen smiled. That's how she wanted to be, too. She reached for her apron and felt glad to be part of the quiet, sleeping house.

Dr. Mike loves the smell of my biscuits, thought Colleen as she quietly got out the flour sack. Her day is going to be filled with complaining folk. She might as well have a cheerful breakfast to get started.

Colleen cut out the biscuits and placed them on the tin sheet, then popped them into the oven.

While they were baking, Colleen added fresh water to the wild iris bouquet in the cracked cup sitting in the table's center. She shook out the quilted place mats and got glasses and plates.

I love my own bed, my own kitchen, thought

Colleen as she swept up crumbs from the counter. It must feel so nice to finally know which kitchen and bed will be yours for the end of time.

" 'Morning, Colleen," Sully said, walking in from the barn. "Little ahead of schedule, aren't you?"

Colleen smiled and shook her head. " 'Morning, Sully. I guess the sun and my worries woke me up early." She got two blue coffee mugs from the hooks. "Is Dr. Mike feeling all right?"

Sully nodded as he rinsed his hands. "She's fine. Long hours sap your strength. Once home, even the strongest warrior has to hang up his armor."

Colleen added water to the coffeepot and spooned in the grounds. "I don't understand."

Sully picked up a piece of bread and spread some butter on it. "Michaela never likes you children to be unhappy."

Colleen sighed. "I'm sorry I've been upset lately."

"You have been fine, Colleen. But with the clinic demanding so many hours, Michaela feels guilty when she sees unhappy people at her own home. She can't help but wonder if she's putting her patients before her family."

"But she doesn't," insisted Colleen.

Sully nodded. "I know. Dr. Mike is just tired."

Colleen wiped her hands on the tea towel. "What can I do to help?"

"You're already helping, Colleen."

"What else can I do, Sully?"

"I guess the only thing any of us can do is to keep our own problems at bay for another week or so. Michaela's plate is pretty full right now. She doesn't need another problem to solve."

Colleen nodded. Sully was right. Dr. Mike had dark circles under her eyes, even when she first awakened.

"Dr. Mike has been working too hard," agreed Colleen. "She needs four hands instead of two."

"She'll be fine if we all back off and let her rest a bit," said Sully.

"With any luck, the grippe will leave town before the May Day festival begins," added Colleen.

"That's the spirit, Colleen," Sully said cheerfully. "Your biscuits smell awfully good. Any jam left from last night?"

"If Brian didn't eat it all," laughed Colleen. "Coffee will be ready soon. I'll go wake Brian. Maybe we can let Dr. Mike sleep in a little bit."

"Did I hear my name?" Dr. Mike yawned as she tied her robe and entered the kitchen. "Something smells wonderful!" She walked over and put her hand on Colleen's shoulder. "Good morning, Colleen. Thanks."

"You're welcome," Colleen said, pleased to see how happy Dr. Mike looked. "Sit down. Coffee is just about ready."

Sully pulled out a chair. "I'll get Brian up."

Colleen set the coffeepot on the table. "No, let

me, Sully. You two sit down and talk."

Dr. Mike reached out and grabbed Colleen's hand as she hurried past. "Colleen, wait. Can you sit down a minute? I'd like to talk to you."

Colleen caught Sully's eye, then pulled back her hand. "I . . . I'll get Brian. It takes him forever to get out of bed. Besides, Dr. Mike, things are fine this morning."

Dr. Mike studied Colleen's face. "I've been so busy at the clinic lately, but if you'd like to talk, I could walk you and Brian to school. Some ladies from the church are taking turns sleeping over at the clinic and a few more hours wouldn't matter."

"There's nothing to talk about, really." Colleen smiled to prove her point. She got the sugar bowl down from the shelf and set it on the table. Colleen was glad when Dr. Mike picked up the coffeepot and poured two cups. Even after a good night's sleep, Dr. Mike was still swallowing yawns.

Colleen hurried up the stairs and rattled Brian's door. "Time to get up, Brian. Breakfast!" Downstairs she could hear Sully's deep voice, then Dr. Mike's laughter. Colleen smiled. Good, things sounded normal. And that's how she wanted to keep them. No matter what happened, she wasn't going to bother Dr. Mike with any silly problems till the clinic was empty. Talking could wait.

11

"Come on, Colleen. Stop picking all those flowers and race me to school," begged Brian.

Colleen shook her head. "I want to pick a few more flowers, Brian. You go on ahead." Colleen added another wild iris to her bunch. She took a step into the tall grass and snapped two lavender locoweeds. Her plan was to keep the flowers in a can of water during school, and then stop by her mother's grave on the way home. She glanced around the meadow. There were so many wildflowers, it was almost like being in a painting.

Ten minutes later, Colleen rounded the hill and found Becky pacing back and forth at the fork in the lane. She had an aspen branch that she was swatting from side to side.

"You're wearing a rut in the road, Becky," Colleen said calmly. She handed her some white columbine. "Happy almost May Day."

"Happy nothing! Wait till you hear!" Becky tossed the branch and flower on the ground. "Wait till you hear what Alice is up to now!"

Colleen bent down and put the columbine back in her bouquet. "I don't care."

Becky tossed back her braids. "Oh, I think you'll be interested in this little story."

"Blake kissed Alice." Colleen kept walking.

Becky skidded to a stop. "Hey, that was my big news. Who told you?"

"We're going to be late for school. Come on, Becky."

Becky ran to catch up. "Golly, Colleen, how can you be so calm about it? As soon as I heard, I wanted to ride over to tell you about it. I still *refuse* to believe it." Becky kicked a stone into the grass. "I mean, Alice had to have *grabbed* him and kissed him, or something like that. I wouldn't be surprised if she tied him up first, blindfolded him, and *then* kissed him."

Colleen shrugged. "It's none of my business."

"It's *everyone's* business!" sputtered Becky. "You're probably wondering how I found out. Listen to this. Susie and her mother came over to our place last night to get some golden lady-slipper seeds." Becky patted Colleen's arm. "Ma saved some for Dr. Mike. Anyway, you know how Susie can't keep a secret. Within five minutes she told me the whole thing. Susie said Blake is *crazy* about Alice. He just went and kissed her and then tried to kiss her again!"

"Well, of course that's what Alice is going to say."

Becky shook her head. "Susie said Alice is considering on whether or not Blake will be her fella."

"I don't care."

"You don't?" Becky leaned forward and stared into Colleen's face. "Not even a little?"

"No. At first I did. Brian told me."

"How did he find out?" asked Becky. "He's just a little kid."

"A little kid who happened to be up in a tree and saw the whole thing."

Becky giggled. "Gosh, I would have loved to have seen the whole thing."

"Why?" The anger in Colleen's voice surprised her. "I mean," she began again, "Blake has every right to court Alice if that's what he wants. It's none of my business. I just think that it would be the polite thing to do if he *admitted* that he liked her, instead of . . ."

"Instead of telling us that he doesn't," finished Becky. "I agree."

"So, let's just ignore them both," concluded Colleen.

Becky patted Colleen's arm. "Very grown-up approach, Colleen."

"They will make a great king and queen," added Colleen.

Becky nodded. "Maybe they'll get married and have lots of little princes and princesses." Becky sighed. "Sometimes it's hard not to be jealous. How come people like Alice end up getting everything?"

"I'm not feeling a bit jealous," insisted Colleen. Yet, as she entered the schoolyard and saw Blake sitting on the front steps, laughing and running his fingers through his hair, she had to admit that she did feel something. She would miss walking home with Blake and listening to his stories. She would miss feeling his strong hand on her arm as he helped her over Mr. Harris's fence.

Reverend Johnson came outside and rang the school bell, drawing the students inside. Colleen stepped back, waiting until Blake got up.

Colleen glanced to the right and studied the blue spruce grove. It had been years since she and Becky had played hide-and-go-seek in there. And now . . . Colleen looked away. Why did she feel betrayed? After all, Blake wasn't sweet on her. If he wanted to like Alice, that was his right. Alice seemed mean to Colleen, but maybe she was so nice to Blake he didn't notice how she treated the rest of the world.

"We'll talk at lunch," Becky promised. "I want to tell you about the lace collar my mother sewed on my dress last night. It is so beautiful."

Colleen nodded, remembering with sinking regret that she still had to find a dress for Saturday. She had grown at least three inches since last spring. What if nothing in the trunk still fit?

Colleen hurried inside and slid into her seat, pulling out her books. She was glad when Reverend Johnson started class. She kept her eyes straight ahead, ignoring the bright red bow that dangled from Alice's curls.

"Put your books away, children," Reverend Johnson instructed. "We have a visitor. Miss Dorothy is going to teach us how to dance!"

The rest of the morning flew by as Miss Dorothy took the whole school outside for dance lessons. Colleen and Becky grabbed ribbon streamers and ducked and raced around the Ponderosa pine that stood for the Maypole. When the next group of dancers took their places, Colleen sat under her favorite tree, a huge aspen. She leaned against its trunk and looked up into the quivering, dancing leaves.

"You know why the aspen is always trembling, don't you?" Blake flopped down in the grass beside her.

Colleen wanted to glare at Blake, to tell him that she was really not in the mood for one of his stories. But as soon as she looked into his eyes, she forgot why she was so mad.

"The leaves aren't trembling," said Colleen. "They're dancing."

Blake shook his head. "No, sorry there Miss Cooper, but that is not the correct answer." Blake stuck a long piece of grass in his mouth. "No, the aspen is cursed."

Colleen narrowed her eyes and studied the dancers. The old Colleen would have been caught up with his teasing, asking him for the true story. Colleen sat up straighter and folded her hands. Let Blake go tell his stories to Alice.

"You in church or something?" Blake sat up and copied Colleen.

"Don't make fun of me," snapped Colleen. She unclasped her hands and, not knowing what to do with them, folded them in her arms.

Blake laughed. "I'm just teasing, Colleen. Sorry."

Colleen turned and studied Blake's face. *Was* he teasing her?

"I just thought you might be interested in the legend of the aspen tree, that's all." Blake yawned noisily and stretched out. "Used to be a time when a certain young lady *loved* listening to my stories, great as they are."

Colleen smiled before she remembered she didn't care a thing about Blake Russell anymore.

Blake crossed his hands behind his head and closed his eyes. "Let me know when Miss Dorothy wants me to help teach the other kids how to dance."

Colleen didn't answer. Blake opened one eye, then the other.

"You're really mad at me about something, aren't you?" Blake sat up. "Is it because I let Brian hold the knife? I got it back from him, okay?"

"It's not that," said Colleen.

"What is it then, Colleen? Talk to me. I thought we were friends."

"I did, too! Which is why I couldn't believe you didn't tell me the truth. You could have trusted me, you know." Colleen's voice was too high; she was talking too fast.

Blake's eyes suddenly clouded over, as if a fog had overtaken him. He sat up, then stood. "Trusting somebody doesn't mean you have to tell them everything about your life, Colleen. Especially some parts that you are trying your best to forget."

Colleen sighed. She felt like saying, Well, you're a big strong guy. If you didn't want Alice kissing you, why didn't you just push her away?

Blake glanced down at Colleen. "I was going to tell you one day, Colleen. I really was."

Colleen stood up, dusting off her skirt. Blake's voice was so cold, sounded so far away, like he was never planning on being close to her again.

"It's none of my business," Colleen said quietly. "Keep your secrets. I really don't care."

Blake's head jerked back, as if Colleen had suddenly slapped his face. The fog grew thicker then, enveloping Blake so completely that the person staring so coldly back at Colleen was a total stranger.

12

Dr. Mike rubbed her eyes and added two more glasses to a tray filled with medicine. Within the last four hours, she had sent home two patients and admitted three. Fortunately, most of them just needed fluids and quinine to settle their stomachs. All of them said they were worried about spreading the grippe and preferred sleeping at the clinic, under the watchful eye of Dr. Mike.

"Why don't you go sit out in the sun for ten minutes, Dr. Mike," suggested Maudie McCoy. She set a tray containing a large pot of chicken rice soup on the table. "Hank won't mind if I'm a little late going back to the saloon. Lunch is already on the stove."

"Thanks, Maudie, but I'm okay," insisted Dr. Mike. "But I do appreciate your keeping us supplied with chicken soup. And yesterday's vegetable stew was wonderful."

Maudie waved away the compliment, but her face glowed. "I'll stop by later with some bread and jam. Let me know what you think of my new jam recipe. I'll be selling jars of it at the festival on Saturday."

Dr. Mike picked up the medication tray and headed up the stairs. With any luck, the clinic would be empty by Saturday and the whole town could enjoy the festival. Dr. Mike stopped halfway up, suddenly remembering Colleen's festival dress. She was going to have to find time to go through the trunk with Colleen tonight. She shifted the tray to her other hip and continued up the stairs, turning into the first room on the left.

"Are you feeling any better, Loren?" Dr. Mike set down her tray and handed him a glass of quinine water.

"No, I'm *not*," he muttered. "I don't have time to be sick, Dr. Mike. I have things to do."

"You seem back to your old self," she said with a grin. "I know this is a busy time for you at the store."

"Busy ain't a big enough word to describe it," he snapped. "Seeds coming in, ribbons for the May Day, and every day another frantic mother wanting to buy another yard of fabric for those fool dresses. Reverend Johnson could have asked *me* before he planned all this nonsense. What are we doing celebrating an English holiday anyway? We're never going to end up being admitted as the thirty-eighth state if we're having a big hullabaloo about England. Not that anybody asks me.

No, sir. I would have spoken right up and said we should be having a festival to celebrate the fact that the cross-country road is finally finished."

"Drink this," Dr. Mike ordered. "Try to get some rest."

"Ha!" Loren drank the bitter liquid and then allowed Dr. Mike to pull his covers up. He scowled. "Nice sunny day like this and I'm stuck in bed."

Dr. Mike glanced out the window, smiling at the sunshine. The sun was always shining in Colorado. Sully told her that you could expect a guaranteed three hundred days of sun a year. Perfect weather for her wildflower garden.

"Another pretty day," said Dr. Mike. "Sully drove me into town early this morning and picked up five more packets of seed from the store, Loren. Things are going fine over there."

Loren frowned. "I find that hard to believe. Dorothy said she was going over to the school this morning to teach those kids how to dance." He pulled the covers up another two inches. "Leave me here to die alone."

Michaela laughed. "You'll be out of here by tonight if you want, Loren. Your fever's gone, and you're holding down food. Get outside and enjoy the sun."

"I don't see no reason to smile with me lying here," grumbled Loren. "And I only ate one small bowl of soup. I am a foot away from death's door."

Dr. Mike patted his hand and picked up the medicine tray. "You are *miles* away, Loren." She started to hum as she headed for the door.

"What are you so all-fired happy about?"

"Oh, I was just thinking about the lovely present Sully gave me."

Loren grunted. When Dr. Mike didn't offer any more information, he gave a loud, irritated sigh. "Well, are you going to *share* this surprise, or do I have to feel left out? I don't have any energy to spare, Dr. Mike. I can't be prying facts out of you."

Dr. Mike turned and smiled. "Sully has designed the most wonderful *bird pond* for me, with beds for wildflowers and . . ." Dr. Mike stopped, startled by the immediate reaction from Loren. His whole face seemed to cave in. He put a trembling hand over his eyes.

"Loren, are you all right? What's wrong?" She picked up his wrist, and was alarmed by the racing pulse.

"Sorry, it's . . ." Loren stopped.

"Take a couple of deep breaths," Dr. Mike ordered.

Loren removed his hand, and shook his head. "It's okay, Dr. Mike. I guess just the mention of the bird pond just flung me back in time. For a second there, it was my own Abigail, laughing and bustin' to tell me quick all about the bird pond Sully was making *her*."

Chills raced down Dr. Mike's arms and spine. Abigail? Had Sully originally designed the pond for his first wife?

"Did . . . when . . ." Each word stuck in Dr. Mike's throat. "Sully didn't mention . . ."

Loren drew in a deep breath and closed his eyes. "Sully never finished it. Once Abigail and the baby died, he just stopped. That's when he left to go live in the wilderness."

Dr. Mike forced herself to listen, forced herself to pick up the empty glass and give Loren one final pat on his trembling hand. She didn't know how long it took her to blindly find her way down the stairs and rush out the door. She felt the sun on her face, then the dry tightness as her tears dried into salty tracks on her cheeks. Why would Sully do this? How could he have given her a present designed for his first wife?

Sully was wrapping his old dreams around her.

Dr. Mike kept her eyes closed for a long time. What did she expect? Was she still so stubborn about wanting that fairy-tale life, the life she had waited for for so long? Maybe she had waited *too* long. Medical school and a practice had eaten away at her twenties. She was living a life made up of Charlotte Cooper's children and Abigail's dreams.

Dr. Mike opened her eyes. She had to get back to the clinic, to her work. Her tears wouldn't change a thing, and fairy-tale endings only came in a book.

13

"What on earth did you say to Blake?" asked Becky, sitting down next to Colleen under the aspen.

"I don't want to talk about it," said Colleen. "I should have kept my big mouth shut. Blake is furious with me."

Becky rolled her eyes. "His fury has spilled out over the whole class, Colleen. He almost got in a fight with Richard over which one would play Robin Hood, and he told your little brother to keep his crummy hands off his knife."

"Blake yelled at Brian?" Colleen groaned. "Brian will be crushed. He adores Blake."

Becky giggled. "Alice tried to see what was bothering him, and he told her to leave him alone."

"Told me the same thing." Brian stood in front of Colleen, his shadow as dark as his face. "Blake said I should go sit with you since you're so worried about him being a dangerous influence."

"What?" Colleen scrambled to her feet. "I never

said that." She reached out and took his hand. "Brian, Blake and I had a little disagreement, but I never said anything about you. He's mad at me, not you."

Brian pulled his hand away. "You had to say *something* to get him that mad." He looked back over his shoulder at the group of boys surrounding Blake. "Told me to go sit with you and Becky before I skinned a knee." Two tears slid down Brian's cheeks. "I ain't no baby."

"Blake's the baby!" snapped Colleen. How dare Blake hurt Brian, just to get back at her? What kind of monster was he?

"Go play with Petey," suggested Becky. "You two can climb trees."

Brian shook his head. "He's watching Blake carve." Brian's gaze traveled to the hillside. Blake had five or six younger boys surrounding him.

"Tomorrow you can bring your own knife and carve me something," Becky suggested again. "I would love a hook like you did for Dr. Mike."

"Ma won't let me have a knife," muttered Brian. "Not old baby Brian."

"Dr. Mike sees more accidents," said Colleen.

"It ain't fair." Brian's head jerked up as the boys on the hill started to laugh. "Ma doesn't know everything, just 'cause she's a doctor."

Colleen reached out and took Brian's arm. "Listen, Brian. Ma is real busy at the clinic. Don't you go worrying her, you hear?"

Brian shook off her hand. "Everybody treats me like a baby."

"Well, *act* like a big boy, then," suggested Colleen.

Brian took a step back. "I do, Colleen. I'm big enough to do what I want."

Colleen watched as Brian raced into the schoolhouse.

"He'll be okay," said Becky. "Nobody likes getting teased."

"Yeah," Colleen agreed slowly. "I hope Blake is happy."

"There you are," snapped Alice. "Busy talking about me?"

"Heavens no," cried Becky. "We're trying to have fun, not make ourselves sick."

"Very funny, remind me to laugh!" Alice crossed her arms and frowned at Colleen.

Colleen stared back at her, then turned to go. "I want to go check on Brian."

"Wait a minute," snapped Alice, stepping in front of her. "I have a *bone* to pick with you."

14

Michaela saw Sully walking toward the clinic as she stood at the upstairs window. He was grinning as he walked.

"Hey, Jake!" he called as he passed the saloon. "Tell Maudie I'll be by for some soup soon as I talk to Dr. Mike."

Michaela let the curtain drop and turned back to Mrs. Potts. "Now, I want you to drink as much of this as you can, to get the fever down."

Mrs. Potts nodded. "My head feels like someone shot me full of buckshot, Dr. Mike."

"You'll feel much better tomorrow."

"Dr. Mike!" Sully called up the stairs. "Is there a doctor in the house?"

Mrs. Potts eyebrows went up. "Sounds like the groom is looking for his bride."

Michaela's lower lip quivered at the word *bride*. Which bride was in Sully's thoughts today?

"Hey," Sully said softly from the doorway. "Can

I talk to you for a minute? How are you feeling, Mrs. Potts?"

"Terrible," she said, mustering a smile. "I remember when my husband lured me out to Colorado, he said, "Honey, the weather is so nice out there, they had to hang someone to start their first cemetery."

Sully laughed. He looked at Dr. Mike. "I have a little something for you, Michaela, if you have a minute."

Dr. Mike moved to the bed next to Mrs. Potts and began fluffing up the pillows. "Actually, I don't right now, Sully. I need to get this bed ready, and make sure Mrs. Potts is getting enough fluids, and . . ."

"Oh, don't worry about me," insisted Mrs. Potts. "I'll sip my glass full of magic. You go talk to that handsome husband of yours."

"It will only take a minute," Sully added.

Dr. Mike ran her hand along the already smooth sheet before slipping out of the room.

As soon as she was in the hall, Sully took Michaela's hand. "Close your eyes."

Michaela cleared her throat. "Sully, can't this wait? I am up to my elbows in duties."

Sully's smile faded. "What's wrong? Are you feeling all right?"

"Yes," she whispered. "I am running a clinic here, though, and I can't take time for tea with you."

Sully let her hand go. "I wasn't asking you for tea, Michaela." He reached into his pocket and drew out a small brown package. "I thought it might cheer you up."

Dr. Mike glanced up at Sully, not quite sure of what she was feeling. She unwrapped it slowly, pulling back the paper and unrolling the soft white padding around another small box. "What is it?"

"Open it," said Sully. His smile was back.

Inside the box was a small porcelain square with MY LADY'S GARDEN printed in small lavender letters.

"We can hang it from the tree above the wildflower garden. Or I can find a way to fit it into the side of the bench."

"It's lovely," Dr. Mike said softly. She drew in a deep breath and felt tears stinging. "Where did . . . where did you get it, Sully?"

He put his hand on her cheek. "It's a secret."

Michaela closed her eyes, unable to keep the warm tears inside any longer.

"Michaela, what's wrong?" asked Sully. He put his hands on her shoulders, but she shook them off. "Tell me what's bothering you."

Michaela cleared her throat, then pressed the small porcelain gift back into Sully's hand. "Put this back, Sully. I don't want it."

"What?" Sully's eyes filled with confusion. He stared down at the sign. "What am I supposed to do with it?"

Michaela shrugged as she quietly slipped by him. "Put it with your other keepsakes, Sully."

Michaela opened the linen closet and pulled out a stack of clean towels. She held them to her pounding heart, waiting. Finally she heard a clatter, then the quick, steady pounding of Sully's footsteps as he hurried down the stairs and out the clinic door.

Michaela turned, blinking back fresh tears. As she neared the steps, she saw the glint of something pearly white on the floor. Bending down, Michaela fit together three pieces that read MY LADY'S GARDEN. She brought it closer and studied it again, the delicate lavender writing becoming a pastel blur through her tears.

15

"**A** bone to pick with *me*?" Colleen stared at Alice. What possible problem could Alice be inventing now? Wasn't it enough that she was a shoo-in for May queen, and had Blake Russell crazy about her?

"Your little brother is telling all his shrimpy friends that he saw Blake and me kissing in the blue spruce grove."

Colleen shifted her feet, hoping Alice knew exactly how *bored* she was with the inquisition. "He saw what he saw."

"Exactly." Alice glanced over her shoulder at Reverend Johnson talking to Miss Dorothy. "But I don't know if Reverend would be too thrilled with the news. And if Miss Dorothy hears your brother talking about it, she might just go and tell my mother."

"Horrors!" cried Becky, pretending to fan her face. "And would your ma think that just *maybe* you weren't the perfect little person she raised?"

"The point *is* I am not going to risk getting in any trouble, and being kicked out of the May Day festivities. So, Colleen, please tell your little brother to *keep his big mouth shut.*"

"Tell him yourself," snapped Colleen.

"You're in charge of him," replied Alice. She grinned and jerked her chin back toward Blake. "Blake just told us that he thinks you would feel better if you could keep Brian on a *leash.* A very short leash, so Brian won't trip and get dirty."

"Blake said that?" Colleen's heart bolted so far forward that it almost flew out of her mouth. Not a single word sounded like Blake.

Alice nodded. "Ask him yourself."

Becky scowled. "Why don't you go drown yourself in the well, Alice?"

Alice laughed and walked away. Becky reached out and grabbed onto Colleen's hand. "Don't let her get you mad, Colleen. With any luck, Alice will wake up turned to stone like Sleeping Ute Mountain."

Colleen nodded, then started to laugh. "What are you talking about?"

"The other day, Blake told me this *great* story about the Ute tribe. Seems like there weren't that many of them, but they were all as large as mountains." Becky shuddered. "Glad they don't go to school here. Anyway, these mountain Ute guys were real hotheads, like our own darling Alice. That tribe was always starting fights. One season

100

they went north and left one tribesman to guard their village. Said they would be right back, but of course they weren't. Blake said he heard they were *so* obnoxious up north that the gods shrank them. Tried to teach them a lesson. So now we have these little shrinky hotheads running around. After a century or two, the poor sentry gets tired and goes to sleep. By the time the little Utes arrived back home, their sentry had turned to stone." Becky pointed to the mountains. "And there you go."

Colleen shook her head. Wait until she told Dr. Mike Becky's latest story. Dr. Mike was entertained by Becky, saying she didn't always make sense, but she had a heart bigger than any found in an illustrated medical book. Too bad you couldn't look up *personal* problems in one of Dr. Mike's books.

"Becky, I'm not sure of the point you're trying to make."

Becky blinked, surprised. "The *point* is, don't let Alice get you so mad that you end up doing something that would really mess up your life. Blake said you can learn a lot from the Indians, even the hotheaded Ute Indians."

Colleen sighed. "The only thing I'm learning from Blake is that I don't understand him at all anymore. It's hard to decide when to talk to somebody about a problem, and when to just ignore it and hope it goes away."

"I have tried to ignore Alice O'Connor since I was six, and she's still here."

Colleen stood up. "Miss Dorothy is leaving. Let's go over and say good-bye."

"Thank you for coming," Reverend said as he shook Miss Dorothy's hand. "The boys and I will assemble the Maypole tonight after school, and perhaps you could come tomorrow for one final rehearsal."

"I would be delighted to help," Miss Dorothy assured him. She turned and waved at Richard and Blake. "And boys, be sure and stop by Mr. Bray's store if you want any more help with the skit. I like what you've written so far. Blake, you are terrific as Robin Hood. Have you cast Maid Marian yet?"

"I'll be Maid Marian," Susie called out.

"You're a Maypole dancer," Reverend reminded her.

"I'll be her," offered little Caroline.

Reverend smiled. "Maid Marian has to be just a little taller and older, Caroline. But I could use your help in passing out columbine plants."

"Can I pass out roses instead?"

"Well, the columbine was discovered by a man named Edwin James about fifty years ago. He didn't live too far from here. I thought it might be nice to use a flower discovered by a neighbor." Reverend looked over at Richard. "The festival is just around the corner, boys. You need to pick

102

someone for the part right now so she'll have time to rehearse. I want a tip-top skit."

Richard looked over at Blake. "The other day you said *you* had the perfect Maid Marian, Blake."

Blake nodded. "I know."

Richard grinned. "Well, big guy. Don't keep us all in suspense. Who did you pick?"

"Colleen."

"What?" cried Alice.

"Excellent," Reverend said, starting to clap.

Miss Dorothy joined in and Becky tried to whistle. Within minutes, the only three people not smiling about Blake's choice were Alice, Blake, and Colleen.

16

"You will be a perfect Maid Marian," Becky said on the walk home from school.

"I don't *want* to be part of Blake's skit," complained Colleen. "And now I need a second dress for the festival. This whole May Day is ruining my favorite season."

"Want my mother to help find you a dress? She has a real pretty yellow one with tiny lavender flowers. You'd look beautiful in it."

"Thanks, Becky. Maybe I can stop over after school tomorrow."

"Or I could bring it to the rehearsal tomorrow night."

Colleen's eyes widened. "That was a joke, wasn't it? Reverend would never allow a midnight rehearsal in the woods."

"I don't think it was a joke. Richard said he found out about it in a book. The night before May Day, the young people in the village would gather in the woods and collect hemlock and flowers for the festival." Becky smiled. "It sounds like fun to me. We're all supposed to bring food and blankets so we can have an English snack around the campfire."

Colleen shook her head. "There is no way we are going to be allowed to wander around the forest with Richard and his crazy friends."

"But Richard read about this!" cried Becky. "Reverend should be proud of him for doing such good research. It's in a book, Colleen."

"So was bearbaiting, Becky."

Becky scowled. "You're ruining all the fun, Colleen. At least say you'll ask Dr. Mike if you can go."

"Yeah," Colleen said slowly. "If I ever see her."

"Well, I'll talk to you tomorrow, Maid Marian," said Becky, stopping at the fork in the lane. "And I'll just bring my mother's dress to school tomorrow. We're running out of time, Colleen."

"Thanks, Becky. See you tomorrow."

As Colleen headed up the lane, she peered ahead for Brian. He had bolted from school so fast, she hadn't had a chance to catch up with him.

"Colleen, can I talk to you?"

Colleen jumped as Blake stood up from behind a huge timberline tree. "I didn't see you."

He walked toward her and extended a folded sheet of paper. "Sorry about sticking you with the part of Maid Marian."

"Are you sure you want me to have it?"

Blake looked embarrassed, scratching his head. "It's just a skit, nothing grand."

"Right."

Blake shoved his hands into his back pockets. "Richard has a midnight rehearsal planned for tomorrow night. Everyone is supposed to meet in the huge piñon grove by his pa's barn."

Colleen nodded, remembering the day years ago when all the local kids raced through the thousand-year-old grove, eating so many of the tasty piñon nuts that everyone went home sick.

"I can't believe Reverend agreed to that." Colleen wondered if Dr. Mike and Sully would allow her to go.

Blake grinned, looking for a second like the Blake Colleen remembered. Relaxed, full of fun. "Richard didn't exactly check with Reverend Johnson. He just told him that we would be rehearsing well into the night."

"It's going to be pretty dark at midnight."

"Everyone is to bring a lantern. We can hang them in the trees. Kind of like that fairy tale where . . ." Blake stopped, scratching his head again. "Well, there's your part. I wrote it myself the other day, so it isn't too good."

Colleen's fingers tightened around the folded script. "Okay."

Blake started walking. "We might as well walk together, since we're going the same way."

"Might as well." Colleen's mouth felt so dry,

she could barely swallow. Whatever happened to the fun she and Blake used to have together? Where does that fun go when it leaves a relationship? Colleen sighed with the weight of another question she'd never find the answer to.

Blake stopped, swinging his head so quickly that Colleen dropped her skit.

"Listen, you don't have to walk with me," snapped Blake. "You're acting like we're walking the longest mile or something."

"What did I do?"

Blake gave an exaggerated sigh.

"I . . . I wasn't sighing about anything you said," insisted Colleen.

Blake held up both hands. "I give up, Colleen. I totally give up on trying to understand you. Ever since you found out about Beth, you've been acting like I'm some sort of a monster."

"Beth?" Colleen asked. Blake's old girlfriends were nearly as meddlesome as the current one. "I don't care about Beth. But I think you're crazy for getting mixed up with Alice."

Blake stopped. "What are you talking about?"

Colleen stopped. "What are *you* talking about?"

"When Beth died, our whole family kind of fell apart," Blake said carefully. "We moved here. My pa said when a chief died, the whole tribe would move to a new area, no matter how good the hunting and streams were." Blake swallowed. "So we came here to start over. To try to forget." He shook his head. "How in the world did you even find out about her?"

"Blake." Colleen put her hand on his arm. "I'm sorry about Beth, but I don't know what you're talking about. What did I find out?"

Blake's face went pale. "I . . . I thought you heard about my little sister dying."

Chills prickled down Colleen's arms. "I never knew you had a sister."

Blake rubbed his hand over his mouth. "I should have kept my stupid mouth shut."

"I won't tell."

Blake started walking faster. "Great. My pa finds out about this and we'll be packing again."

Colleen hurried to catch up. "Blake, why would I tell anyone? You can trust me."

Blake stopped. Picking up the end of his shirt, he wiped at his face. "It was all my fault. Now *this* is all my fault."

"Dying isn't anyone's fault," insisted Colleen. "My ma died because a rattler bit her. Sully's wife died trying to have a baby. Dying is what happens sometimes, Blake."

Blake lowered his shirt. "Well, Beth was only seven years old, Colleen. She wasn't supposed to die yet."

Colleen's eyes burned. Blake looked so sad, she had to turn away.

"Beth's birthday was coming up and she kept asking for a pony. Pa said maybe next year."

108

Blake stopped and drew in a deep breath. "So, one day I was walking home from school and I found these two little puppies crying and running around the roadside. I brought both of them home for Beth. One died that night, but Beth carried the other one around night and day for a week. She wouldn't let anyone else tend to it. Even when it started falling down every time it tried to walk. Beth would just scoop it up in her arms."

Blake went to the side of the road and sat. He just sat in the tall grass, staring at his hands.

Colleen didn't know whether to ask him to continue or not. She hated talking about her own mother dying. Talking was like poking the cooling coals, making the smoldering fire turn back into the red-hot flames, like it was happening all over again. So Colleen just sat down beside him, in the tall grass, and didn't say a word.

"The puppy had rabies," Blake said finally. "We didn't know it. I thought a rabid animal would be foaming at the mouth. Doc said Beth got rabies from the puppy licking her fingers, her skinned knees."

Colleen's throat tightened. She couldn't imagine life without Brian. "It wasn't your fault, Blake."

"I brought the puppy to Beth," he said bitterly.

"And she loved it. You didn't know."

Blake sighed. "So, my parents will move us to a place where nobody knows again. Where nobody will give them that sad look."

Colleen picked at the threads along the edge of her skirt. "I won't tell anyone, Blake. I promise you that."

Blake didn't even answer.

"And I won't give you a sad look."

Blake shook his head. "Stories have a way of surfacing, Colleen. No matter how hard we pile the dirt on top."

"Well, it's nobody's business until you're ready to tell them."

Blake nodded. "Thanks." He turned and gave her a small smile, his own eyes red. "Beth was nice. You remind me of her."

Colleen smiled.

The two of them sat in the grass, swatting gnats, watching the butterflies. Blake finally stood up.

"I really thought you knew," he said, as they started walking again. "What were you talking about when you mentioned secrets?"

Colleen bit her lip. Kissing Alice seemed so insignificant when placed next to Beth's death.

Blake gently elbowed her. "Hey, I'm sick of secrets, Colleen."

"Me, too." She tried to collect her thoughts, but finally just dumped the whole bag out in front of Blake.

"Brian saw you kissing Alice."

Blake hooted. "He did?"

Colleen stopped in the middle of the road. Blake

didn't seem the least bit embarrassed.

"He was up in a tree, and he saw you," continued Colleen.

Blake grinned at Colleen. "Well, he didn't see it proper then. 'Cause I didn't kiss Alice."

"He *saw* you!" Colleen couldn't believe Blake was sliding back into a lie.

"Alice kissed *me*," corrected Blake.

"What?" Colleen started to laugh.

Blake nodded. "She said she had to tell me something private. Then she thanked me for taking the blame for her." Blake rubbed his chin. "Am I leaving anything out?"

"Blake!"

"Then she kissed me." Blake laughed. "She's been following me around ever since. Keeps asking me if I want her to bake me a cake. I swear, that girl is harder to shake than a burr on a burro."

"So Alice kissed *you*," repeated Colleen. "Wait till I tell Becky."

Blake groaned. "Putting it in the *Gazette* would keep it more private."

Colleen smiled. She felt so light inside, she almost flew.

"Did I ever tell you how the Colorado burro became known as the Rocky Mountain canary?" asked Blake.

"No," said Colleen. "But we have another quarter mile to go. Why don't you tell me now?"

Blake stuck a piece of grass in his mouth and

nodded. "Seems that there was this burro . . ."

Colleen held her books tighter, hoping they would keep her heart from pounding too loudly. She felt so good, as if she were part of the rainbow after a sudden storm. With every breath, she was once again smelling spring.

17

After Blake went his way, Colleen raced the rest of the way home, anxious to talk to Brian and start supper. Brian was busy in the barn, with a barrel shoved up against the door.

"Brian, let me come in," said Colleen. "Why do you have the door blocked?"

"I'm working on a surprise," he hollered back. "I'll be in for supper pretty soon."

When she went inside, Sully was already stirring something in a black pot.

"Hi," he said. "Mrs. McCoy loaded me up with a jar of her chicken soup. She said that with Dr. Mike working so hard, she figured we'd all like a break."

"Is Dr. Mike coming home for supper?"

Sully shook his head and shrugged. "I don't know."

"Did you talk to her today?" asked Colleen.

Sully banged the lid on the pot. "I went to see her, but she wasn't in the mood to see me."

"It's those long hours," Colleen reminded him.

Sully nodded. "Something is eating her, all right."

"Ask her what it is." Colleen got three bowls from the shelf. "I know you don't want us bothering her, Sully, but I think it's plumb unnatural to stop talking to someone just because they're busy."

"She has a full plate already, Colleen," said Sully. "And I won't be adding to her problems right now."

Colleen set the silverware down. "Sorry."

Sully came over and put his hand on her shoulder. "Sorry. I didn't mean to snap. I lost my temper once today. I shouldn't be doing it again."

"Sully, there's going to be a rehearsal at Richard's place tomorrow night. Can I go?"

Sully was staring out the window. "Fine with me. Check with Dr. Mike."

Colleen smiled. Maybe she would be able to go. Dr. Mike was so busy, she wouldn't have time to worry.

Brian came inside and went over to the basin to wash up.

"How's your surprise?" asked Colleen.

"What?" Brian spun around, his hands dripping water onto the floor.

"Brian, watch what you're doing," said Colleen. She bent down and wiped up the water. "What's wrong? You look like you've seen a ghost."

"Noth . . . Nothing," stammered Brian.

"So what time does the rehearsal start tomorrow?" asked Sully. He set the black pot down in the center of the table.

"You gonna go to Richard's rehearsal?" asked Brian. "I didn't think you'd be going to that!"

Colleen glanced over at Brian and shook her head.

Sully started to ladle the soup into the bowls. "The festival is Saturday, Brian. Not too much time left."

Brian grinned as he slid onto the bench. "Can I go, too?"

"No," said Colleen. She set a basket of bread in front of Brian. "It will be too late."

Brian pushed away the bread and put his head down on the table. "Shucks!"

Sully ruffled his hair. "Hey, maybe we can go night fishing tomorrow, Brian. We haven't done that in a while."

Brian raised his head. "Okay. That will be more fun than sneaking around in the woods with Richard and Becky and the other kids."

Sully looked over at Colleen. "I thought you said it was a rehearsal?"

"It is," said Colleen. "But it's a late one. It starts at almost midnight."

Sully sat down and picked up his napkin. "Don't even ask your ma about that, Colleen. That's too late."

"Lots of kids are going," said Colleen. She glared at Brian for opening his big mouth.

"Don't get mad at me," said Brian. "Besides, now you know how I feel. I never get to do anything big." Brian leaned over and pulled on Sully's shirt. "Sully, you just have to talk to Ma about lettin' me use a carvin' knife. I'm the only one at school not able to try to make the Maypole top. Kids are callin' me a baby. And Blake said he'd . . ."

"Your ma said no, Brian."

Sully looked up at Colleen. "Will Reverend Johnson be at this midnight rehearsal, Colleen?"

"No," Colleen admitted.

"Then we won't even mention it to Dr. Mike." Sully picked up his spoon, then let it clatter to the table. "Okay, let's ask the blessing so we can eat."

Colleen clasped her hands and recited the blessing with Brian and Sully. Their words marched out stiff and cold, as if they weren't a bit thankful for the food before them.

Then all three of them fell silent and picked up their spoons to eat the soup that none of them felt like eating.

18

After the supper dishes were washed and dried, Brian went back out to the barn. Sully said he wanted to check on a fence, and Colleen went into her bedroom to go through a trunk. She didn't really care about a dress anymore. She was glad Blake wasn't cross with her, but the air hanging in her *own* house was getting chillier and chillier. It didn't feel a bit like spring inside.

Colleen pulled a pale rose-colored dress from the trunk. It had been her mother's Easter dress many years ago. Colleen shook it out, running her hands over the soft cotton. Her mother had looked so pretty in the dress. She had worn a soft scarf of pink and dark green, tied at the waist. Colleen bent down and rummaged through the trunk. She pulled the scarf from a tangle of belts and ribbons.

This will be fine, thought Colleen as she held the dress up in front of her. I can borrow one of Dr. Mike's cloaks, and I'll look exactly like Maid Marian.

At the thought of Maid Marian, Colleen remembered the poem she was to recite. She laid the dress across her bed and picked up the folded paper Blake had given her.

Colleen grimaced as she picked it up. If Blake wrote this for her days ago, had he been mad at her? Things had been so confusing lately, Colleen wasn't quite sure when she and Blake had stopped being friends. The important thing was that *now* they were back to being friends, and she wasn't about to let anything get in the way of their *staying* friends. Wild horses couldn't pull the story about his little sister's death from Colleen.

On this special May Day,
baskets fill with buds and holly.
Greetings from Robin Hood
are plentiful and jolly.
Robin likes to right all wrongs,
in Sherwood Forest and the town.
'Tis time for May dancers to begin
their prance with ribbons round and
round.
A king and queen will soon be
crowned!
Yet no one rules what Robin's found.
Three cheers for all who gather here!
Ten cheers more for Robin's Marian
dear.
No queen shines brighter

in this fold,
Marian wears no crown,
but her heart is gold.

Colleen lowered the page, smiling. Robin Hood was crazy about Maid Marian. Did that mean that Blake was crazy for Colleen? Dr. Mike would know. Colleen hurried out of the room. And to think that she had spent all those days worrying that Blake liked Alice!

It wasn't until Colleen was standing in the empty kitchen that she remembered. Dr. Mike wasn't there. Colleen turned and went back into her room. She folded the poem and put it on her dresser, then hung the dress and scarf on a hook.

She got out her schoolbooks and walked back into the kitchen. She would have to go get Brian soon and tell him to hurry up and start his homework.

Colleen pulled out a fresh sheet of paper and opened her geography book. She flipped through the book and found her page, then closed the book. She didn't feel like doing homework. She felt like talking to someone. She missed talking to Dr. Mike. She was so busy lately between the clinic and Sully, it was hard to find time for talking.

Colleen picked up her pencil and wondered whom she could talk to at this late hour. Brian and Sully were both in a dark mood, and Dr. Mike might not be home till morning.

April 30, 1873
Thursday night

Dearest Ma,

I just found out that Blake Russell likes me. He didn't come right out and say so, but he had Robin Hood tell me. I wish I could tell you everything that has been happening to me lately, but — well, you aren't here. I *miss* you so much it hurts. Like right now. I have good news to tell you, but it won't start being good until you know. You are the best mother in the world and I love you very much.

Colleen folded the note, then walked into her room and slipped it inside the worn pocket of the rose dress. She yawned, then grabbed her sweater. She'd better get Brian, before he could fall asleep in the barn. But before she left the room, Colleen got Blake's poem and reread it one last time. Dr. Mike always said that part of the magic of spring was so many beginnings occurring at once. Buds opening, birds hatching, people shaking off the winter coats and making new friends. Colleen put the note away and smiled. Once she read this at the festival, the whole town, including Miss Alice O'Connor, would know that Blake and Colleen were setting off on a new beginning.

19

Early Friday morning, Colleen came into the kitchen to find a note from Sully propped against the sugar bowl. It explained that he needed an early start to finish an important morning chore. Colleen dressed quickly, fed the chickens as Sully requested, and then awakened Brian. She had an important morning chore as well. With so much going on, Colleen had never made it to the cemetery with her flowers. It would be nice to pick some fresh wildflowers and take Brian with her to their mother's grave. Maybe a silent prayer together would make them both feel better.

"Why are you heading out so early?" asked Brian. He took another bite of his jelly bread and then yawned, mouth half full. "And why did I have to eat my breakfast while we walk?" Brian yawned again. "Did Ma come home last night?"

"No. She will probably be home when we get back from school," said Colleen, swallowing a yawn herself. It was so early that the grass was still soaked with dew. "Brian, finish your jelly bread so you can hold my books. I want to pick some flowers for Ma."

Brian smiled. "Can we take them to the clinic right now?"

"The flowers aren't for Dr. Mike, Brian. They're for Ma's grave."

Brian's face fell. "Do I have to go? I don't like the cemetery." Brian tossed his bread on the ground. "Don't make me go there, Colleen."

"It's a sign of respect, Brian," explained Colleen. "We won't stay long."

Brian glanced up at the sky. "You don't think Ma's sore that I love Dr. Mike so much, do you?"

Colleen shook her head. "Ma's happy you love Dr. Mike."

Brian smiled. "Okay, then. I'll go. I guess I was afraid Ma could read my thoughts at the cemetery. Know what I'm thinking."

Colleen bent down and kissed Brian.

"Hey," cried Brian, looking around quickly. "Don't go kissing me where the fellas can see you! What'd you go and do that for?"

"Because you are so grown up, Brian."

Brian's face lightened. "I am?"

"Yes. It took a real grown-up boy to tell the truth about why you didn't want to go to the cemetery."

"You won't tell anybody, will you?"

Colleen shook her head. "I'm the best secret-keeper in town, Brian."

Colleen and Brian gathered up an armful of wildflowers and headed for the small cemetery behind the church. The only sounds came from the birds high in the trees.

Colleen led the way through the maze of head-stones. When she found Charlotte Cooper's, she knelt down, placing the flowers against the narrow stone.

"Do I have to say my prayer out loud?" asked Brian.

"No." Colleen folded her hands. "I'll say mine silently, too. But I think you should kneel down."

"Does the prayer get delivered faster if you kneel?" asked Brian.

"Faster than a peregrine falcon!"

"Wow." Brian dropped to his knees, moving as close as possible to his sister.

The two children were just getting to their feet when Dr. Mike came slowly out of the church and saw them.

20

"**Ma!**" cried Brian. He raced across the cemetery and flung his arms around her waist. "What are you doing here?"

Dr. Mike hugged him, then raised her eyes to study Colleen's face. "I wanted to say a prayer before I headed for home. I think the grippe has finally left Colorado Springs. Mrs. Potts is the last patient." Michaela ruffled Brian's hair. "You forgot to brush this mop this morning, Brian."

"Colleen woke me up when it was still dark!" He grinned up at her. "I ate my breakfast outside, just like Taffy."

"Where is Sully?"

"He left a note," explained Colleen. "Said he had something to do."

"So," began Dr. Mike slowly, glancing at the mound of flowers on Charlotte's grave. "What brings you two out so early?"

"We brought flowers for Ma's grave," said Brian.

"That was thoughtful," said Dr. Mike.

"Colleen thought of it," said Brian.

Dr. Mike unwrapped Brian's arms and smiled. "You two better get to school now. I didn't bring the buggy, or I'd offer to take you."

"That's okay," Colleen said quickly. "You go on home and rest."

"I will." Dr. Mike pulled on her riding gloves. "And I'll go through my trunk, Colleen. We still have to find a dress for you."

"Don't bother. I found one last night," said Colleen. She wanted Dr. Mike to go home and relax, not rush into another chore.

"You did?"

"One of Ma's old ones," Colleen said. "It will be fine."

Dr. Mike nodded. "Well, I guess you've taken care of everything."

"Just about," Colleen said cheerfully. She wanted to rush up and hug Dr. Mike herself, to tell her that she missed her so much she could barely stand it. But Dr. Mike looked so worn out that a brisk breeze might knock her over.

Dr. Mike smiled, then walked back toward the clinic.

"Ma doesn't look too happy," commented Brian. "You don't think she's sore that we brought Ma flowers and not her?"

Colleen took his hand. "Of course not. Dr. Mike

is just tired, that's all. If something was bothering her, she'd tell us."

"Right," agreed Brian. "Like when she tells me not to burp at the table."

"Right. And she doesn't like me to wear out my eyes by reading when the candle's too low."

"Race you to school," suggested Brian.

"Let's go," cried Colleen.

The children were over the hillside before Dr. Mike had swung the first leg over her horse. She couldn't see them, but she couldn't stop thinking about them either. Spring was a time for new beginnings, yet Sully, and now the children, were tied to the past.

How often do they come and visit Charlotte's grave? Michaela wondered as she rode slowly out of town. Colleen's a young woman herself now. I thought one reason she has been so quiet lately is because of the changes going on within her. I know now it's because she misses her real mother so much.

By the time Michaela arrived home, she could barely keep the tears in. She put her horse in the barn, fed him, and then walked slowly into the house. She glanced around the clean, well-scrubbed kitchen. Sully and the children were managing quite well in her absence. She picked up Sully's note and read it. Sully hadn't mentioned any new project he was working on. Unless . . . Michaela wondered if Sully was still working on her bird pond and garden. She crumpled the note and left it on the table. She didn't want that project completed. It had stopped being hers the moment she found out it had once belonged to Abigail.

Dr. Mike made a fresh pot of coffee and wandered around the house, too tired to sleep. She put fresh sheets on Brian's bed, then went into Colleen's room to strip her sheets as well. It had been weeks since she had time to catch up on laundry. As she was leaving Colleen's room, she noticed the pale rose dress hanging on the back of the door.

This is pretty, thought Dr. Mike, but it looks too big for Colleen. Surely I have a dress in my trunk that would work better.

Michaela smiled for the first time that morning. She took the dress from the hook and draped it over her arm. When Colleen came home from school, there would be an even fancier dress laid across her bed.

As Michaela stepped out of the room, a folded square of paper bounced off her foot. Bending down, Michaela picked it up and unfolded it.

April 30, 1873
Thursday night

Dearest Ma,

I just found out that Blake Russell likes me. He didn't come right out and

127

say so, but he had Robin Hood tell me.
I wish I could tell you everything that
has been happening to me lately, but —
well, you aren't here. I *miss* you so much
it hurts. Like right now. I have good
news to tell you, but it won't start being
good until you know. You are the best
mother in the world and I love you very
much.

Michaela's cheeks flushed, and the tears she had
tried to hold back spilled down both cheeks. Colleen must feel so terribly alone to sit down and
write to her dead mother.

Michaela refolded the note and put it back into
the pocket of the dress. Next, she carefully re-
placed the dress on the hook. Wearing her mother's dress was probably the only way Colleen could
still feel close to her mother, thought Michaela.
She touched the dress, sighed, and quietly closed
the door.

21

Reverend Johnson had just unlocked the door and was warming up the schoolhouse with a light fire when Colleen and Brian walked in.

"Well, good morning," Reverend said, looking pleased for the company. "Are you all set for the big festival tomorrow? We're all to meet in front of the church at ten o'clock."

When Blake arrived at school, he acted shy, almost embarrassed around Colleen. He was showing a few boys how to carve a teacup handle, and when Colleen walked by, he said, "So, what did you think of the poem?"

Colleen tried at first to keep her smile small, but it just kept going till it went from ear to ear.

Blake ducked his head, then smiled himself. "I'm glad you liked it."

"Liked what?" Alice had appeared from nowhere. She was as quiet as a barn cat.

"I wrote Colleen a poem to read tomorrow," Blake said easily.

Alice's eyebrows went up under her bangs. "Well, isn't that sweet?" She smiled at Blake. "Would you write me a poem, too, Blake?"

"I already did!"

"You did?" Colleen and Alice cried at once.

"He did," repeated Alice, smirking at Colleen. "My very own private poem." She rubbed her hands together, practically licking her chops.

Blake pulled a small square from his pocket. "I hope you like it. I mean every word."

Colleen stared at Blake. How could he do this? Didn't yesterday mean anything to him? Maybe she had been wrong about the poem. How many games did this boy play?

Colleen could feel her cheeks blaze as she watched Alice unfold the poem and begin to read.

I hope she *doesn't* read it out loud, Colleen thought miserably.

Alice looked up from her poem and stared straight at Blake. Her eyes narrowed. "You . . . you . . ." Alice stopped, swallowed, and then crumbled the note into a tight ball, thwacking it against Blake's forehead.

Richard and Paul started to laugh. Blake blinked, then grinned at Colleen. He bent down and handed the crumbled ball to her. "Here, a little souvenir."

Colleen's hand closed around the poem. She went back to the cloakroom and smoothed the paper.

ROSES ARE RED,
BLUE SPRUCE ARE BLUE,
ALWAYS REMEMBER
WHO KISSED WHO!!

Colleen covered her mouth as she started to laugh. She folded the note, then slipped it into her pocket. Blake was so funny.

"What are you smiling about?" Becky stood in front of her, holding a brown paper package. "Here, my mother said you could wear her yellow dress."

Colleen reached for the dress. "Oh, Becky, thank you. You are the best friend."

"Of course," agreed Becky. "Now tell your best friend what is so funny."

Colleen showed Becky the note.

"So what's funny about that?" asked Becky.

"Because Blake didn't kiss Alice, she kissed him!"

Becky grinned. "So I was right. But how did you find out?"

"Blake told me yesterday. We had the greatest talk. We talked for over an hour!"

Becky grabbed Colleen and gave her a hug. "I am so glad you two are friends again. So tell me everything. What did you talk about?"

Colleen paused, wondering what she could share with Becky.

"Well, just start at the beginning," Becky urged.

"I will, but . . ." Colleen squeezed the package. "He told me that Alice kissed him. To thank him for taking the blame for the note."

Becky started to smile. "Okay, and what else?"

"That was about it." Colleen turned and set the package on the shelf above her coat hook.

"You said you talked for over an hour," reminded Becky. "So, what else did he say?"

Colleen shook her head. "Maybe it wasn't an hour. That's about all."

Becky's face froze, then settled into a stranger's face. "That's about all you want to *tell* me, right?"

"Becky!" Colleen reached out and took her hand. "We just talked about a few other things. Kind of pri . . ." Colleen stopped in midsentence, but it was already too late.

"Pri-vate things," finished Becky. She hung up her sweater and turned to leave. "Well, I don't need to hear any of that. Save that for your best friend."

"You *are* my best friend," insisted Colleen. She could see how hurt Becky was. Becky was chewing her upper lip. She only chewed it when she was trying not to cry.

"We'd better sit down," said Becky. She shook her hand free from Colleen's and left.

Colleen pressed her forehead against the wall,

wondering why everything always had to be so complicated.

"Class!" called Reverend Johnson from the main room. "Come on, it's time for what we've all been waiting for! Let's have those elections for May queen and king!"

Colleen slipped out of the cloakroom and into her seat. Becky shot her such a cold look that she shivered. As Reverend Johnson laid a voting paper on her desk, Colleen knew for a fact that her best friend, Becky Binder, would not be voting for her today!

Caroline Beecher raised her hand. "Excuse me, please. But how do you spell Blake?"

As everyone started to laugh, Alice flew out of her seat. "Here, Caroline, I'll show you how. In fact, let me print it for you!" Alice tried to lower her voice, but Colleen heard as she asked, "Do you want to know how to spell Alice?"

Colleen turned her eyes toward her own paper. She printed Blake for king. She ran her pencil along the line to queen, but couldn't continue.

"Oh, go ahead and vote for yourself," hissed Becky.

Colleen shook her head. "I don't even want to be queen."

"I'm going to vote for you," Becky said with a frown. "But I'm still mad. Why can't you tell me what Blake said?"

"Girls!" Reverend stood at the front of the classroom, frowning so deeply that his eyebrows formed a furry path across his forehead.

Colleen ducked her head, pretending to finish with her ballot. She knew she deserved to be scolded. She and Becky had been whispering much too much lately. But Becky was the only one she was free to talk with. And if she didn't talk to someone, Colleen felt she would just explode.

Colleen was glad that Reverend kept a cold eye on her the rest of the afternoon. It made whispering to Becky impossible. And the truth was, she couldn't explain things to Becky. She had promised Blake she wouldn't tell a soul about his sister, Beth.

Colleen picked up her pencil and wrote her own name down for queen. Becky elbowed her and grinned. Colleen smiled back. May Day was tomorrow, and Colleen could hardly wait for it to be over!

22

When Colleen and Brian got home from school on Friday, Dr. Mike was sitting at the table with a cup of tea. It was wonderful to have her home again.

"Hello, welcome home!" cried Colleen. She bent down and gave Dr. Mike a kiss on the cheek.

Dr. Mike nodded. "Thank you. I'm hoping Mrs. Potts will go home in the morning." Dr. Mike yawned. "Excuse me. So, how was your day?"

More than anything in the world, Colleen wanted to sit down and tell Dr. Mike exactly how confusing everything was. She wanted to tell her about Blake's poem, and Brian being heartsick over not being able to carve, and how being May queen seemed so far away and unimportant. . . . Colleen looked up. Dr. Mike was staring out the window, like she was already someplace else.

"School was okay. We voted for king and queen."

Brian nodded. "I voted for you and Blake, Colleen."

"I found a dress to wear for Maid Marian," said Colleen. "And Mrs. Binder said I could wear hers for the May queen contest."

Dr. Mike sat up straighter. "You can't borrow a dress, Colleen. It isn't proper."

"Sure I can," said Colleen. "Becky's my best friend."

Dr. Mike stood up quickly and rinsed her cup in the basin. "Surely I can find you something to wear from among my dresses."

Colleen shook her head. "That's all right. I like Mrs. Binder's dress." Colleen wanted Dr. Mike to relax.

Dr. Mike kept her back to Colleen for a long time. Finally she nodded, and walked past her and into her room. She closed the door quietly, but it had all the impact of a slam.

"What's wrong with Ma?" asked Brian.

"She's tired," Colleen answered automatically. She stared down at the brown paper package, wondering why Dr. Mike didn't even want to see it. She didn't seem a bit interested in Colleen's running for May queen.

"Maybe I should give her my surprise now," suggested Brian. "To cheer her up."

Colleen slumped down on the bench, tired herself. "I was just thinking, Brian. If you give Ma the hook, she'll ask if you carved it, and then she'll find out you used Blake's knife."

"But she'll see I didn't get cut at all!"

Colleen nodded. "Well, I used to think that. But now I'm wondering if Ma will just be mad."

Brian leaned against Colleen. "So, what should I do? I painted it and everything."

"Let me think about it," said Colleen. Suddenly she looked up. "You did give Blake back his knife, didn't you?"

Brian nodded, then shook his head.

"Brian, did you or did you not give Blake back his knife?"

"Well, I gave it back, but then he asked me to hold it this morning, since you guys were friends again, and . . ."

Colleen groaned. "Give it to me, Brian."

"I'll give it back myself!"

"No, give it to me now!'

"You said I was big this morning. I guess I'm big enough to carry it to school tomorrow."

"Tomorrow is Saturday. Now give me the knife!"

Dr. Mike's door opened so quickly that it nearly flew off the hinges. "What are you two fighting about?"

Colleen put her arm around Brian's shoulder. "Nothing. Sorry to wake you."

"What did you say about a knife?" Dr. Mike

crossed her arms and walked closer. "I told you not to carve, Brian."

"He watched the older boys carve, mostly," said Colleen.

"Guess what, Ma. Sully said maybe I can have a knife come Christmas," Brian said quickly, eager to change the subject.

Dr. Mike rubbed her eyes. "Well, we will see."

"I'll start supper," Colleen said. She grabbed her apron off the hook. "Brian, go get me a pail of milk, okay?"

Brian was out the door in a flash. Dr. Mike watched Colleen get out the flour.

"Colleen, is there anything I can do to help you with May Day tomorrow?"

Colleen shook her head. "No. I'm fine."

Dr. Mike nodded, then went back inside her room. Even though supper was ready within the hour, Dr. Mike didn't come to the table. Sully tapped on the bedroom door and went in, and when he came out, his face was as pale as the biscuit batter.

"Is Ma all right?" Colleen asked.

Sully said yes. But he slid into his seat and then stared out the window while Brian asked the blessing. Colleen had to ask Sully twice to pass the corn, and when she asked him how he liked his sausage, he glanced down at his plate as if he had forgotten it was there.

Colleen and Brian exchanged worried looks. It

seemed things couldn't get any worse at home. There was a frost covering just about every sentence spoken. As Colleen passed Brian the bread, she had a terrible thought. What if Dr. Mike found the knife before Brian had a chance to return it?

Colleen glanced outside, glad it was already dusk. In another few hours, it would be pitch-black outside. Dark enough for her to hurry over to Richard's and return Blake's knife. She would be back in plenty of time to get ready for May Day. Maybe the first day of May would bring happiness back into their house.

23

Colleen asked Brian for Blake's knife twice after supper. He said he would give it back himself. Colleen sighed, wondering if she should trust Brian to return it before the festival started. She wished she could tell Sully or Dr. Mike, but the tension in the house, the closed doors, and the weary looks made Colleen feel as if she were walking on eggshells.

Colleen tried on both the Maid Marian dress and the dress that Mrs. Binder had loaned her. Neither fit her very well, but she managed to tuck in the extra cloth with a scarf and a belt.

Colleen turned in front of the mirror, running her hands down the sides of the rose dress. Her hand slid across the note she had written the night before. Colleen took it out and reread it. Maybe she should give it to Dr. Mike. It might make her feel better. Suddenly she had a great idea. She would ask Brian to add his greeting. They could put it in Dr. Mike's May basket tomorrow morning. Colleen opened her door carefully. Sully and Dr. Mike had started off on a walk a few minutes earlier.

"Brian?" Colleen hurried across the floor. She tapped on his bedroom door. "Brian, open up. I want you to sign something."

Colleen pressed her ear against the door, then opened it.

Brian was not in his room. His window was open, and the cool night breeze billowed his curtains in and out.

"Brian?" Colleen called again. She left her letter to Dr. Mike on the bed and tried to think if Brian had gone on the walk with Dr. Mike and Sully. No, because Sully practically had to force Dr. Mike to walk with him. He convinced her finally by saying he had something very important to show her. Something that wouldn't wait.

Colleen stuck her head out the window, wondering if he could be back in the barn. The barn was dark. The entire yard was dark except for the circle of light surrounding Sully's large lantern hanging by the front porch. As Colleen pulled her head back in, her hand brushed a piece of paper from Brian's desk.

*I have gone to return something. I will
be right back so don't get mad or worried.
Don't yell at Colleen cause she told me
to return this a long time ago.*

Brian

"Brian!" Colleen dropped the note and raced
down the stairs. It was after nine o'clock. When
had Brian disappeared? She stood in the middle
of the kitchen, chewing her thumbnail and trying
to think. Would Brian have walked all the way
over to Blake's house? Colleen didn't think he
would. He had never been there himself, and
knew only that Blake lived beyond Richard's
farm.

Richard! Colleen grabbed her sweater. Brian
knew all the boys would be meeting at Richard's
later for the midnight rehearsal.

Colleen grabbed a piece of paper, scribbled *be
back soon,* and flew out the door. It would take
her at least ten minutes by horseback to get to
Richard's house. With any luck, she would pass
Brian on the way and bring him back before they
were missed.

Colleen could see the lanterns glowing from
the piñon grove before she left the main road.
She had not passed Brian along the road, but
he had probably taken a shortcut through the
meadow.

"Oh, Brian, this is the dumbest thing you've

ever done," muttered Colleen as she dug her heels into Taffy's sides.

As Colleen got closer, she could hear Richard and Blake laughing. Paul and two other boys from the school were sitting on logs, but she couldn't see or hear Brian.

"Halt, who goes there?" boomed Richard. He had a blanket thrown over his arm and was holding a tree branch as if it were a sword. "Identify yourself, or I will be forced to run you through with my sword."

Colleen hopped off her horse and led him into the clearing. "It's me. I'm looking for Brian."

Blake stood up, looking around. "He isn't here."

Richard marched toward Colleen, swaying as he came.

"Well, and we thought none of the ladies would be present at our midnight rehearsal."

"I can't stay," said Colleen. "I'm trying to find Brian. I thought he might have come to return your knife, Blake."

Richard pretended he was twirling a moustache. "Methinks you really came to see me, Maid Marian. Admit it, cast off thy deceptive cloak and . . ."

"I have to find him *now*," cried Colleen. She looked around. "Brian, if you're here, you'd better come out now!"

The night was still. In the distance Colleen heard the howl of a coyote.

"He's probably back home by now," said Blake. "Want me to ride with you?"

"No," cried Colleen, feeling the panic begin to rise like creek water. "He has to be here."

"Well, he *isn't*," insisted Richard. "Relax, he'll show up. Listen, Colleen, while you're here, watch this." Richard hopped up on a log balanced between two huge walls of rock. "Okay, pretend I'm Little John, and now Blake, you pick up that stick and try to knock me off the log."

Colleen turned her back on him and headed back toward her horse. She would have to go home and tell Sully and Dr. Mike, no matter how mad they got.

"Get out of my way, Little John!"

Colleen froze, then spun around. Brian was on the log, brandishing his own stick.

"Brian, didn't you hear me calling?" Colleen dropped Taffy's reins and headed over. "Get down from there."

Brian turned and flashed Colleen an impish grin. "I told you I wasn't a baby, Colleen."

"Dr. Mike and Sully are going to be worried sick unless we get home right now."

"Okay." Brian tossed his stick down and reached in his pocket, pulling out Blake's knife. "Bet I can hit that tree, Blake!"

Blake and Colleen called out at the same time, "Brian, stop!"

Brian drew his arm back as he wound up for the throw, just as Richard reached out a hand to grab the knife.

"Don't!" Colleen cried again.

Brian shot Colleen another victorious grin and then, before Richard's hand could touch Brian's, the log rolled and both Brian and Richard toppled forward into the blackness.

24

Colleen started screaming before she even saw the blood.

"It's okay," Blake said automatically, as he grabbed a lantern and raced over to the log.

"Brian!" cried Colleen. "Brian!" Why wasn't he crying?

Blake lifted his lantern, sending a pale umbrella of light over Richard and Brian. Colleen glanced quickly at Richard, her heart quickening at the sight of his arm. He was holding it at an odd angle.

"I'm hurt," cried Richard. "I busted my arm."

Colleen crouched down and moved closer to Brian. He was staring back at her, his eyes huge with fear.

"It's okay." Colleen echoed Blake's words. "Brian, tell me what hurts."

Brian shook his head, sending tears down his cheeks. Finally, he glanced down at his leg.

Colleen's stomach lurched. Sticking out of Brian's upper leg was Blake's knife.

"Oh, my gosh," muttered Blake, lowering the lantern.

"Pull it out!" cried Brian.

Richard leaned forward, grimacing as he held his arm closer. "Hey, stay calm, Brian," Richard said softly. "Look at me. I busted up my arm and I'm just sitting here."

Brian started moaning then. A low, animal sound.

"Brian, listen to me," said Colleen slowly. "You are going to be all right. Paul, go get Dr. Mike. Ride fast."

Another boy moved in with a lantern. Brian closed his eyes and the moaning got louder.

"Get me a blanket," ordered Colleen. "Richard, are you okay?"

Richard nodded. "Yeah, stick with Brian. Why is he making that noise? It's starting to spook me."

"Pull the knife out, Colleen," suggested Blake. "Or should I?"

Colleen stopped his hand. "Don't touch it. It's not bleeding too badly right now. If you pull it out, it might rip open an artery."

"What . . . what are we going to do?" Richard looked wildly around the grove. "My pa can't see us from the house. I don't even know if he's back from the barn yet."

"Dr. Mike will be here soon." Colleen gently placed a blanket around Brian's shoulders. "Blake, put this blanket around Richard."

"I'm okay," said Richard, but he allowed the blanket to be draped around him. "Colleen, I swear, I had no idea your little brother was here."

Colleen shook her head. "It's okay. Brian, listen to me."

Brian opened his eyes, but they didn't seem like Brian's eyes then, in the darkness, with blood seeping into the cloth of his trousers around the handle of the knife.

"I'm leaving the knife in until Dr. Mike gets here," Colleen said calmly. "It won't hurt for it to be in your leg for a little bit longer. It's keeping your veins pushed together, which is good." Colleen licked her dry lips and wondered what else she could do. It was important for Brian to remain as calm as possible so he wouldn't go into shock.

Brian started to whimper. "Ma's gonna be so mad."

Colleen nodded. "First she'll fix you up, then she'll be mad."

"Listen," said Blake. "Brian, look at me a second."

Brian's eyes looked to the left and right, and finally focused on Blake's face. Blake slowly knelt, bringing the light down with him. "Did I ever tell you about the time my pa was driving the stage up one of the steepest peaks in Colorado?"

Brian reached out and grabbed onto Colleen's hand. "Pull it out, Colleen. It's burning me."

Colleen held tightly to Brian's hand. "Just another minute, Brian."

"It's burning hot!" shrieked Brian.

Colleen looked up at Blake, then over at Richard.

"Paul's probably at Dr. Mike's right now," Colleen said cheerfully. "I bet she's grabbing her black bag and hopping on the horse."

"So, anyway," Blake continued in a loud voice. "Once my pa got to the top of the peak, he got scared. Probably just as scared as you are right now, Brian."

Brian's eyes darted over to Blake.

"Want to know why?" asked Blake.

Brian glanced down at his leg. He chewed on his lip for a long minute before he looked up again. "Why?"

"Because," said Blake. "My pa knew he had to go back down the other side. His brakes weren't strong enough for a hill that steep. So he got out and tied two huge logs to the back of the stage, and dragged them all the way down the mountainside."

Brian leaned forward. "Really?"

Colleen shot Blake a grateful smile. She pulled the blanket back as more and more blood seeped out from the wound.

"Brian! Colleen!"

Brian burst into tears at the sound of Dr. Mike's

voice. Colleen felt her own eyes sting, but she blinked them back. How was Dr. Mike going to be able to remove a knife embedded that deeply, out here in the piñon grove?

Dr. Mike and Sully were off their horses and by Brian's side in seconds. "Paul caught us as we were coming to look for you. We found notes and . . ." Dr. Mike said quickly, words tumbling out so fast that she was hard to understand.

Dr. Mike bent down and saw the knife. Her hand flew to her mouth, but only briefly. She lowered it and then leaned forward to smile into Brian's terrified face.

"You are a very brave boy," she said carefully. She gently turned Brian's leg. Sully had his knife out before her hand even reached for it. Dr. Mike slit Brian's trouser leg and opened it up. "I need as much light as you can give me."

"Am I going to die?" asked Brian in a small voice.

"No." Dr. Mike pulled the scarf from around her neck and wiped at the blood. "Someone hand me my bag. Things look good. Doesn't look like an injury to either femoral vessel."

For the next five minutes, Dr. Mike worked quickly and without saying a word. Brian started to whimper, and Blake started another story.

"Sully," said Dr. Mike. "You and Colleen are going to have to hold Brian very, very still."

Colleen moved behind Brian and locked her

hands around his arms and chest, while Sully gently held Brian's hips and legs still.

"On the count of three," whispered Dr. Mike.

"One, two — " Dr. Mike drew in a deep breath. "Three."

The knife moved slowly upward in Dr. Mike's hands. Brian started to scream as the knife started to move. He fainted a second later.

25

The sun rose on a clear morning with pink skies and a thousand birds singing.

Colleen got up from the kitchen table and poured Dr. Mike another cup of coffee. Sully was asleep in the chair.

"Is Brian going to be all right, Ma?"

Dr. Mike looked up and nodded. "Yes. We'll have to watch the wound. But I think he's going to be fine. And Richard's break was clean."

Colleen set the pot down on the table. "I feel so bad. I told Brian to give the knife back a long time ago."

"We can talk about it later," Dr. Mike started. Then she smiled. "Actually, we haven't *talked* in a long time."

Colleen nodded. "I know. I . . . I missed you so much. I even wrote you a letter."

Dr. Mike lowered her coffee cup. "You did?"

Colleen nodded. "It's up in Brian's room. I left

it there. That's how I knew he was gone. I saw *his* note."

"Sully and I came back to the house and found *both* notes."

"So you read it?" Colleen sighed. "I wrote it the other day, but I didn't have a chance to give it to you."

"I thought it was written for Charlotte."

"No." Colleen shook her head. "Why would I write Ma?"

"I don't know. I seem to have jumped to every conclusion known to man in the last week." Dr. Mike got up and pulled Sully's blanket up around his neck. She walked back to the table and took Colleen's hand. "My heart was broken when I thought Sully had given me Abigail's bird pond."

"I don't understand."

"Loren told me that Sully gave Abigail a bird pond. Last night, when Sully finally made me tell him what was wrong, I found out that it wasn't true at all."

"Mr. Bray lied to you?"

Dr. Mike laughed softly. "No. A misunderstanding. Sully had started to carve a *birdbath* for Abigail, not a pond with a bench and birdhouses and gardens." Dr. Mike shook her head. "I feel so terrible. I hurt Sully's feelings and . . ."

Colleen reached out and put her hand over Dr. Mike's. "It's okay now. Isn't it?"

Dr. Mike looked lovingly at Sully. "It's fine." She turned to Colleen. "But I haven't had any time for you."

"Sully said you were so busy. I had a thousand things to tell you, but I thought it was best to wait till you were finished with the grippe."

Dr. Mike rolled her eyes. "I think the day we decided to stop talking in this house, we came down with a grippe of our own."

"It spread through the whole house," added Colleen.

Dr. Mike opened her arms. "Come here and give me a hug."

Colleen was out of her seat in a second, wrapping both arms around Dr. Mike. "I missed you."

"Oh, and did I miss you," whispered Dr. Mike. "I love you all so much."

"We love you," said Colleen. "You're the best mother ever."

After a long minute, Dr. Mike patted Colleen on the back. "Come on, it's time to get you ready for the festival."

"Oh, that's all right," insisted Colleen. "I don't even *want* to go. I'd rather stay here with you."

"Nonsense," said Dr. Mike, pulling Colleen up. "We are going to pin you into my best dress, wash and curl your hair, and make you into the most beautiful queen of the May this town has ever seen."

"Will you come watch? Alice will probably win."

Dr. Mike smiled. "You're our queen of the May. Now — I want to hear your lines for Maid Marian, too. Sully told me all about the skit."

"Who will stay with Brian?"

"Sully will. Says he wants to have a long talk with him about the *proper way* to carry a knife."

The sun started to shine in the front windows, sending soft yellow rays across Sully's face.

"We're so lucky, Colleen," said Dr. Mike softly.

"I know."

Colleen and Dr. Mike linked arms and walked slowly toward the window.

"Looks like May is going to be a pretty month," Dr. Mike said.

Colleen nodded. "Did I ever tell you spring is my very favorite season?"

Dr. Mike laughed. "Only a hundred times. But go ahead. Tell me one more time."

"No matter what happens, I'll always remember this spring."

Dr. Mike leaned her head against Colleen's and the two of them watched as the most perfect sunrise of all spread its magic across the Colorado plains.

26

"You look beautiful, Colleen," whispered Dr. Mike as she pulled the buggy up under the shade tree by the church. "My dress looks better on you than on me."

Colleen glanced down at the pink roses printed across her skirt. Dr. Mike had worn this very dress in Boston twenty years earlier. "Thank you so much for helping me get ready. I know Alice is going to win, but . . ." Colleen smiled. "I am just so happy that Brian is okay, and you and Sully aren't upset with each other." Colleen drew in a deep breath. "Ma, I think my May basket is overflowing already."

Dr. Mike laughed. "Maybe you need a bigger basket, Colleen. That's the best part about living. Sometimes things just get nicer and nicer."

Colleen grinned and climbed carefully out of the buggy. "I just hope I don't forget my lines for Maid Marian. Blake is such a good writer!"

Dr. Mike tied the horses to the tree and nodded. "I hope I get a chance to talk to this boy now that the grippe has left our town. He sounds like quite a fellow."

"He is," Colleen said quickly.

"There you are!" cried Becky. She picked up the hem of her long skirt and raced down the hillside. "Reverend is a nervous wreck. Someone tangled up the ribbons for the May dance, and Richard broke his arm and won't be able to speak his part in the skit." Becky leaned against the wagon and sighed. "I think I may have to put on a pair of trousers and pretend to be Richard. How disgusting."

Dr. Mike laughed. "You will do a fine job, Becky. You look lovely."

"Thanks." Becky grinned, then glanced up at Colleen. "Wow. You look beautiful, Colleen."

Colleen smiled back, twirling around to let the full skirt swirl like a carousel. "Dr. Mike wore this to her sweet sixteen party."

"Alice will drop down dead with envy," Becky declared. "Even though she is wearing her mother's best necklace and a jackrabbit cape."

"I bet she looks pretty," said Colleen. She looked across the crowded yard. The whole town was milling around.

Becky giggled. "She's wearing *a lot* of rabbit, Colleen. Let's hope the dogs are tied up."

"Reverend Johnson is calling everyone to attention," commented Dr. Mike. "We'd better go over to the stage area."

Becky picked up her skirt and hurried up the hillside again. "Come on, Colleen. May Day is about to begin."

Colleen turned and threw her arms around Dr. Mike. "Thank you so much for everything. For taking such good care of everyone, and . . ." Colleen hugged Dr. Mike harder. "Thank you for loving me so much."

Dr. Mike hugged her back. "Loving what is gentle and wonderful is a very easy job, Colleen. That is what you and spring are all about."

Colleen stepped back and smiled. "I have a May basket for you at home. I keep adding more surprises, though, and it's overflowing. I guess I have to get it more organized."

Dr. Mike shook her head. "It sounds perfect. A May basket is filled with love. It's supposed to overflow." Dr. Mike smiled. "We can exchange baskets at home. I can't wait."

"Who says you should?"

Colleen and Dr. Mike turned to see Sully walking down the hill. He was grinning and holding a handful of wildflowers.

"Sully!" Dr. Mike glanced around. "What are you doing here?"

"Matthew and Ingrid came over to sit with Brian. I told them I need to wish my best two girls a happy May Day." Sully handed Colleen the wildflowers. "You look beautiful, Colleen."

"Thank you." Colleen kissed Sully's cheek and hurried up the hill. "See you both later."

Colleen turned at the top of the hill, watching as Sully handed Dr. Mike a small box. She opened the lid and drew out a small white disk, smaller than a tea saucer. Dr. Mike reached up and hugged Sully, then kissed him and the little white sign. Colleen smiled as she turned away. In the spring, love came in baskets, boxes, and . . .

"Miss Cooper!" Reverend Johnson grabbed her arm and pulled her toward the stage. "We are waiting, Colleen. I am about to announce the May queen."

Colleen nodded, hurrying to catch up as Reverend raced back across the yard. Colleen barely had time to smile at Blake as she hurried past. As Colleen climbed up onto the stage, she grinned at Becky in the front row, then tried to ignore the scowl Alice was sending her from two feet away.

27

"Thank you for turning out to launch Colorado Springs' very first May Day festival," Reverend Johnson called out across the crowd. "I want to thank the children from the school for their hard work, as well as Miss Dorothy for teaching them all to dance so nicely." Reverend cleared his throat and pulled a sheet of paper from his pocket. "Now, I would like to begin our celebration by announcing the king and queen."

Colleen felt a tug in her stomach. Somehow, standing on stage in front of the whole town made May Day seem a lot more important. She smiled at Becky, then waved at Dr. Mike and Sully, who had their arms wrapped around each other's waist.

"The election was very close," continued Reverend. "But I am happy to announce that Blake is to be king, and . . ."

Applause washed up from the audience. Colleen and Becky grinned at each other. Colleen drew in a deep breath. Maybe being queen would be fun after all. She had so much to talk to Blake about. He had been wonderful with Brian last night, and . . .

"And our beautiful queen is none other than our own Alice . . ." Reverend's final words were clipped by Alice's cries of joy.

"I can't believe it!" Alice shrieked above the applause. She stood before Reverend Johnson as he placed a crown of rosebuds on her head.

"May I present the May king and queen of Colorado Springs to their loyal subjects," declared Reverend Johnson.

Colleen clapped along with the others. She kept her eyes down. Not because she was disappointed; she knew Alice was going to be chosen queen from the start. Colleen just didn't want to watch when Blake kissed her.

"Congratulations, Alice," said Blake.

Colleen sighed. In a minute it would all be over and she could enjoy playing Maid Marian and watching Becky dance around the Maypole. Colleen raised her eyes, hoping they could all leave the stage now.

"Thank you, my king!" cried Alice. She held out both arms to Blake.

Blake reached up and grabbed one of Alice's arms, pumping it up and down. "Have a good day, Alice." Blake turned and hurried off the stage.

The audience started to laugh, then remembered to clap. Alice stomped her foot, and before she had time to close her mouth, a dozen little boys climbed up onto the stage, surrounding her.

"Hey, give us our peppermints!" cried the Olson twins.

"You owe me some candy, Alice!" another boy cried. "I voted for you."

"Me, too. Where's my nickel bag of candy?" hollered Petey McCoy.

Alice held onto her rosebud crown and fought her way out of the tangle of tiny arms. "Get away from me!"

Colleen started to giggle as she climbed down from the stage. Becky reached up a hand to help.

"Her royal majesty is having a bad day," said Becky. "I think the king forgetting to kiss her had a whole lot to do with it."

Colleen nodded. Poor Alice. She got the crown, but not the king.

"I didn't *forget* to kiss the queen."

Becky slapped her hand over her mouth. "Yikes. Sorry, Blake."

Colleen spun around, surprised to see Blake leaning against the stage. "Congratulations, Blake. We . . . we didn't know you were here."

Blake smiled, then bowed. "I just came to pay my respects. Is Brian okay?"

Colleen smiled. "Fine. Matthew is with him."

Blake nodded. "Good. Well . . ." He glanced

over at Becky. "No one told me the king had to kiss his queen."

Colleen felt her face get warm. Why did Becky have to open her mouth? Blake didn't need to go and kiss Alice!

Colleen studied her shoes. She didn't want to watch.

"Happy May Day, my queen." Blake said it so softly, Colleen wasn't sure it was meant for her. It wasn't until he took her hand and leaned forward to kiss her cheek that she understood.

"I . . . " Colleen ran out of words. Instead, she squeezed Blake's hand and watched as he walked slowly off toward the tent by the church. The sun moved out from behind the blue spruce grove just then, sending its warmth and brightness out in every direction.

"Wow!" Becky sighed. "If I had my streamers, I'd dance around you, Colleen."

Colleen grinned, reaching up to touch her cheek. Dr. Mike was right. May baskets couldn't possibly hold all the magic of spring.

About the Author

Colleen O'Shaughnessy McKenna began writing as a child, when she sent off a script for the *Bonanza* series. Ms. McKenna is best known for her Murphy books, the inspiration for which comes from her own family.

In addition to the eight books in the Murphy series, Ms. McKenna has written *Merry Christmas, Miss McConnell!*, the young adult novel *The Brightest Light*, and *Good Grief . . . Third Grade*, a spin-off of the Murphy series. Ms. McKenna is also the author of another book based on the characters from *Dr. Quinn, Medicine Woman*.

A former elementary school teacher, Ms. McKenna lives in Pittsburgh, Pennsylvania, with her husband and four children.